The Dark Moors

Inspired by Emily Brontë's 1847 novel
Wuthering Heights

By Ally Adams

The Dark Moors

Inspired by Emily Brontë's novel, *Wuthering Heights*
First published in 2021

Atlas Productions
Greenslopes QLD 4102
Web: www.atlasproductions.com.au

A catalogue record for this book is available from the National Library of Australia

Cover images by: cocoparisienne, Brigitte, Gordon Johnson (Pixabay) and from Bigstock and Shutterstock.
Cover design by Helen Goltz, Atlas Productions.

For Emily

I hope you are not rolling in your grave with this adaptation.

Books by Ally Adams

The Saints Team series:

Team Lucas
Team Tomás
Team Niklas
Team Alex – The Russian

Spies in Love series:

My Boyfriend the Spy
I Spy my Guy

Chapter 1 – At the window

Catherine

There's a saying that time makes everything better, dulls the pain. That absence makes the heart grow fonder. My heart is feeling many things, but fondness is not one of them.

How much time does it take to achieve this? I miss him now more than I missed him a year and three weeks ago when he left. It feels just as bad. The only difference is that now I'm angry too, whereas before I was just weepy.

Where are you, Heath?

It is nearly eleven p.m., a school night, but there is no one around to police that anymore. Mum and Dad have gone, and it is just me, Nelly and Hindley in the house. Nelly is the housekeeper, cook, estate manager, you name it. She's been here forever... really, forever. I can't remember a time when Nelly wasn't around. As for the other tenant, my brother, Hindley, he is too busy enjoying hosting his friends here every night to care if I'm home or not – I'm not saying that's a bad thing. I heard them leave about half an hour ago in a couple of cars, so it's just me and Nelly home now. I know most of Hindley's friends, we've all grown up together more or less, even though they are four years older than me. They're all into sport and cars, and girls now, I guess. I was Hindley's pesky little sister until last year, now they're all interested in talking to me. Funny that!

I can barely hear myself think over the howling of the window outside and the rapping on my window panes. It used to scare me as a child, now I find it comforting, like an old friend that visits regularly. For a moment it takes my mind off Heath, but that is short-lived. Are you running away from me or Hindley, both or neither of us? Make contact for God's sake! You're cruel. Do I mean that little to you? Did you give me a thought in the entire year since you walked out of here and disappeared? Meanwhile, I guess you don't mind that I've thought about you every waking moment and dreamt about you as well. Not even a message through a fake online account or a note passed to me at school from a stranger you paid off, I'll take anything! I can think of so many ways to get a message to me, why the hell can't you? I'm looking for signs all the time from you, I'm pathetic. I'm the queen of losers hanging around waiting for the guy I've seen every day of my life since I was a kid to contact me, and Hindley doesn't even give a shit that you are gone or how I feel. Truth be known, he's thrilled you aren't here, he's the only one who is.

Another bang against the window, the branches were beating the glass in a frenzy, another dance of the shadow branches across the ceiling.

I drift in and out of sleep and wakefulness, remembering

you when you first arrived… you were a child, a demon, my stepbrother. Wild and dirty with your soulful eyes that had seen more than Hindley and I could ever imagine. Hindley hated you on sight, I loved you – drawn to you like the earth orbits the sun. You were eight and I was six, and I thought you were the most exotic thing I had ever seen, like Dad had brought home a wild animal.

We promised to be together forever. Come back to me.

The wind is howling again. Thank you, wind, I was getting lost in history then. I closed my eyes to sleep. Go away memories, just give me one good night's rest.

Sleep.

Stop knocking on my window, let me be.

Sleep. Wake, tapping. 'Cathy, let me in.'

'Heath!' I jump up and race to the window to let you in. Pushing and shoving against the wedged window frame until it burst open. Cold air rushed in, the wind was howling, my eyes watered with the cold.

'Hurry, you'll freeze,' I said, and then you seized my wrist.

'Let me in, Cathy, or I will die out here without you.'

'Then come, come in, Heath, come in quickly,' I yelled above the noise of the wind and reached out to help you. But you were gone.

'Heath, show yourself.'

I strained to see you but could see nothing in the dark and fog. The wind swallowed my words.

'You're home, Heath, please,' I yelled, trying to direct you home.

'I'm lost on the moors,' you said again. 'Help me, Cathy.'

Then I woke up gasping, screaming your name. I don't believe it was a dream. You were here. Why would you leave me?

Chapter 2 – Blood types

Catherine

I tried to go back to sleep but gave up after an hour, propped myself up in bed and scanned my phone. My best friend Tilly was up and online and as soon as she saw my profile live, she messaged me.

'Okay if I call?' she asked.

'Sure,' I sent back and grabbed my phone so the ringing didn't wake Nelly, even if she was at the other end of the house. I answered it on the first ring.

'What are you doing up?' Tilly said, forgoing the traditional hello greeting.

'I had a bad dream, and the wind is going berserk here. It creeps me out,' I said, pulling my blanket up around my neck.

She made a sympathetic noise.

'Why are you up?' I asked.

'A lot of drama here,' Tilly said, talking fast, which she did when she was excited. 'Dad's just come home and there's been a murder!'

'What? No!'

'True story,' Tilly said.

This was not good. Our village was a tourist village and things like death scare people which isn't good for businesses like my family's winery and cafe – they stay away.

Tilly's dad was a police sergeant who, with his fellow cops, covered about twelve surrounding areas. But because Tilly's family lived here, he was first on call for the local crimes. Usually, he's dealing with speeding, break-ins, the occasional drug heads and drink driving – a murder was new and kind of exciting!

'Tell me everything you know,' I insisted.

'Okay. Dad's just back now and I'm not allowed to say anything so strictly in the vault...'

'In the vault,' I agreed and made our symbolic sign even though she couldn't see me.

'Well, they think it was a drug deal gone bad. The guy is old, about fifty and had a fair bit of class-A drugs on him... that's cocaine and heroin, I think, anyway whatever, he must have been selling them because he had bags of it on him, no cash though. But his throat was almost torn out, according to Dad!'

'Gross,' I groaned. Tilly loved her gore.

'His wrists were a mess too and there was lots of blood around.'

'Lots of blood?' I said, storing that fact away. I jumped as a tremendous gust of wind outside shook the windows and the tree shadows leapt into the room.

Tilly continued. 'Weird though, that whoever killed him didn't take the drugs he had on him. Dad says they must have taken the money because someone saw him selling earlier and when they found him, he had no cash at all on him. You'd think they'd take the drugs and try to sell them if they were that desperate for cash to kill someone!'

'Too hard, maybe cash is easy,' I suggested. 'Who found him?'

'The guy who does the cemetery ghost tours. He was heading home after the midnight one. Got to go, I can hear Dad coming up the stairs.'

She hung up on me and minutes later, speaking of weird, I got a message from Edgar Linton. Really, wow! Edgar Linton… seriously wow. At school, he'd always been just at a distance – cool, aloof, moody, and gorgeous.

We'd known each other since we were kids, and I knew him better then, we'd grown apart. We were neighbours and our families were business partners, but we hadn't spoken for forever. He was a few years above me at school and always had Charlotte hanging off him. He must have seen me online. Was anyone asleep out there besides the dead guy?

*****

Edgar

Cathy's awake at 2am, she's as bad as me. The last time I checked we both had partners, but I heard Heath had gone and I've jettisoned Charlotte, so timing…

I sent her a quick hello, and she replied.

'Can't sleep?' I asked the obvious.

'Bad dream. And you?'

'No dreams. Are you okay?' I asked.

She sent back a smiley face. 'I am, you're sweet thanks for asking.'

Hell yeah, I'm sweet on her.

'Why are you awake?' she tapped back.

'I'm a night walker,' I joked. I hope she knows that's a joke. I stuck a laughing face in just for good measure. 'Plus, I just heard there's been a murder – a druggie down near the cemetery. Dad got called to take the body to the morgue.'

'I know, I heard too,' she typed with lots of exclamation marks. 'I can't tell you my source though, it's in the vault,' she said.

'Tilly's dad? Don't answer,' I typed back. 'Hey, it'd be great to catch up, it's been forever.' I took a deep breath, released the message, and put it out there. She couldn't have typed a message back quick enough for my liking.

'I'd like that, it's been years.'

I smiled and breathed again.

'Great, I'll message you tomorrow.' Keep it simple and play cool, I coached myself.

'Talk then,' she said. 'Going to get some sleep. Nighty night.'

'Good night, Cathy,' I typed back and watched as her profile disappeared. I put my phone down and laid back, staring at the ceiling.

Our families had been connected for centuries; everyone knows my family's business – Linton Mortuary and Funeral Home, it's kind of an institution in The Moors. It has been around longer than any of the current inhabitants of the town and the generation before that, we probably buried them all too.

I guess not everyone wants their parents to run a funeral home, but I've always liked it... I think it is kind of cool. One day, I'll take over the business of burying the dead and all the perks that go with it – and there are perks and it's all about fluid, yeah, that's our secret.

I've known everyone who works for us since I was born; I used to come to work with my parents when I was a kid, and before and after school. If there was a customer on the premises, the folks would stick me in the back office, but sometimes it was good for clients to see it was a family business. Dad used to say that there's nothing to fear about death and we're here to help people celebrate the lives of their loved ones who have just passed. Yeah, good line.

Most of the time though, the people of The Moors don't care what goes on behind the closed doors of our mortuary; they just hand over their dead and believe that my caring and pale family will prepare the body respectfully for the funeral and burial, and invoice them accordingly. And that's what we Lintons do and we do it well!

This business will look after us both, me and my love. Sure, there had been rumours over the years of blood removed from corpses, but the rumour monger never seemed to stick around long enough to back up their claims – funny that. They must have left town since no bloodless bodies are lying around, murdered. But like all things, that line of thought has taken on this mythical status and was generally ignored unless it was Halloween. It's helped me though... the bullies left me alone at school in case I got my contacts to drain their blood and bury them. Ha, there's a few I'd like to do it too.

Mum and Dad always made a point of inviting anyone in to see how we work if there's was ever any concern and suspicion, and they leave in good health! But few have ever taken up that invitation – and there's no real reason to deal with my family unless you had a dead relative, and then grief overtakes curiosity or so I've heard.

Okay, so about those fluids, coming clean, here goes. The mortuary is the perfect business for my family, a family of generational Sanguineous Immortalis. That's immortal creatures that survive off blood. Yeah, before you freak out, we're not like the vampires you see in movies, we've evolved like all species. The Saps, sorry that's short for homo sapiens – humans – aren't running around hairy with their arms dragging on the ground like apes and neither are we. We're no longer light sensitive or able to be banished with holy water or a crude cross… that's so funny. My sister, Isabella and I, break up laughing every time we watch those old films. Can't believe that used to happen; we get an injection now when we convert and it synthesises… whatever, too boring. Anyway, we're 21st-century creatures and we cleverly survive by being in the right business and contributing to the community. Except for the fact that we're a little pale, you'd struggle to pick us, honestly.

And let's get real… who would miss the blood from the dead? Why bury anything that can be put to good use? What does it matter if a corpse was drained and replaced with fluid before burial or cremation? It's not like they can feel it and who is the wiser?

Besides, embalmed bodies look plumper, a better colour

in death – and my family and our staff are yet to meet a client who doesn't love our work. It's pretty rare anyone wants a closed coffin when their dearly beloved looks so peaceful to view. It comforts them and it gives us a very good supply of blood for ourselves and our clients who needed it. Isabella and I don't need it yet but when the Conversion takes place we will. Then we send the blood over to our business partner, Cathy's family, at the winery for bottling – it's a special blend for those in our village who need it.

As for Heath, yeah, I know he loves her, everyone can see that. I guess that's one redeeming quality he has. But he's moody, unsociable, too rough for Cathy. She needs someone like me.

*****

Hindley

Arrogant bastard. If he's going to sell me stuff at least make it good quality, but that shit is overpriced and dangerous. Bloody drug pusher.

I watched him doing some deals, selling some stuff in one of the side streets in the village. You wouldn't be in that area unless you were dropping off catering stuff or being a scumbag. Then a van cut its light and headed down towards him. This was a more serious buyer; he must have a better product for the big buyers. Sure enough, he pulls out wads of the white stuff. Money's exchanged and it's all over in minutes. He looks around and heads out of the alley. I follow.

He's walking toward the cemetery – perfect, make my day. Dark and not too many there at night, well alive anyway. I stay behind waiting, I'm going to let him see me, that's part of the fun but not until he gets closer to the cemetery. May as well go for the whole chill factor – bloody perfect. It's quieter now and deserted. He's coming to the cemetery gate and there's a sign promoting a ghost tour at midnight. Crap. I glance at my watch – forty minutes until then, plenty of time.

I begin. I let him hear the sounds of footsteps behind him. I pull back into the shadows when he looks back. His heart rate has increased a little. My mouth is watering. I do it again, and he flicks around; not fast enough, he can't see me yet. I can hear his blood pumping now, the beat of his heart like a drum. This is as sweet as it gets, like foreplay before the main act. God, it's a natural high before I drink. I want to feel what the hunt is like – just once and not hunting an animal. I want to feel the adrenaline surging, hear their heart pumping and mine, and have the chase. It seems such an unfair fight with my talent to hunt an animal, they don't stand a chance.

He's walking faster. It's time. I show myself and walk fast behind him. He wheels around again, sees me and continues hurrying, not sure if I'm following him or just heading that way. But now that I'm almost on him, he stops and steps off the path. The cemetery fence runs beside us and no one in there will help him.

'What do you want?' he asks. 'It's you!'

He recognises me as the face in the street earlier. 'I've got rid of all my stuff, you should have bought earlier.'

I grabbed him by the throat and I am salivating with his reactions. His eyes are dilated, his heart is pounding, the adrenaline is surging through him. He's kicking and struggling, but he's no match for me as I push him back against the fence.

'I've got money,' he chokes out the words.

His panic is doing my senses in… powerful, aromatic smell and I can't wait to have him, but I want it to go on longer. I drop him and tell him to run.

'Get the fuck out of my sight or I'll kill you,' I hiss, knowing full well his death was only moments away. He stumbles, and rights himself, and takes off. He's constantly looking back at me and he has to run up the slightly uphill cemetery path.

I can't wait any longer. I take off after him and he screams. The blood, the fear, the power, it's a huge trip. I take him, sinking my teeth into his neck and I taste it as it should be – raw and wild. Oh God, it's unbelievable. He fights me for a while, longer than I thought possible – good job scumbag, but soon he slackens in my arms. I could have drunk him dry but I pull myself off to leave some blood in his corpse or it will look suspicious.

I drop him and stand there, feeling his blood going through me. I close my eyes and enjoy the experience. You can't get this from a bottle or tube. But it's got to be a one-off I tell myself; we all know the rules. We don't do this shit anymore. I look down at the body at my feet. Fucking shame.

'But you were worth it, man,' I said aloud and laugh. 'Right, better make it look like your druggie friends knocked you over.' I lift him like a rag doll, tear his throat so there's a reason he'd lose so much blood and so the bite marks are no longer in his neck. I take the money from his jacket – got to make it look like a robbery, convenient yeah, and I stuff the cash in my pocket. I leave the drugs so they know who his network is, and I make sure he has a bag of powder in his hands… a deal that didn't go down.

I need more blood to put around him. Hmm. I wipe my mouth on my sleeve and quickly head to the office. I don't know what blood type he is, but I grab a bottle of O-type and bring it back. The Cemetery Tour hosts and guests are there now, but on the other side from me. I can see their lanterns making their way through the headstones. I pour some of the blood into the grass around him so it doesn't look like he was drunk dry, but bled out, cork the bottle and I get out of here. That'll be a nice surprise for the tour when it finishes.

My first hunt.

I wish it was Heath lying there dead.

Chapter 3 – A day in the life of...

Catherine

I don't know what time Nelly gets up of a morning but I don't think she ever sleeps in. In seventeen years I've never beaten her to the kitchen of a morning, not once. I haven't tried that hard either, but that's neither here nor there, you'd think the odds were that it might happen a couple of times in all those years. Nope. I could smell toast and eggs cooking.

When I entered, the newspaper was on the table with the murder on the front page.

'Morning, Nelly.' I planted a kiss on her cheek. 'Tilly's dad was called out to that last night.'

She glanced at the newspaper. 'Can you believe it? No good will ever come from drugs,' Nelly said, making a tsk-tsk sound as she returned to stirring the eggs. 'You had a nightmare again, child, your voice carried to my window,' she said with a sympathetic glance as I came to stand beside her. 'And you didn't sleep well by the looks of it.'

The dark bags under my eyes were giving me away. I needed my beauty sleep. If Heath ever did return, my face would send him back to where he came from quick smart.

Nelly poured me a half glass of orange juice and I sat at the breakfast table.

'Thank you,' I accepted it. 'Sorry Nelly, I didn't mean to wake you.'

'Don't be silly, you didn't wake me. I'm an owl, I'm nocturnal,' she said, and I laughed.

'I wondered,' I said. And she gave me a wry look. 'Where's Hindley?' I asked.

'Already left. He's throwing himself into learning that business,' Nelly said.

'Yeah, and he's not making a lot of friends, from what I hear,' I said, and I'd heard plenty. People who had worked happily for decades with Dad were looking for other jobs. 'Hindley rubbed them the wrong way. He walks around the office asking people what they did for their salary and if they were worth it!'

Nelly sighed. 'Your father would roll over in his grave.'

'Well then, he shouldn't have gone to his grave,' I said bitterly.

Nelly piled scrambled eggs onto a plate in front of me.

'That's plenty, thank you, Nelly.'

'You eat like a bird,' Nelly said, and poured us both a cup of tea. She finished and sat opposite me.

'Was it about Heath again, the dream?' Nelly asked.

'It was, but it was different this time,' I explained. 'It freaked me out.'

I blinked furiously and focussed on the scrambled eggs so Nelly couldn't see the tears in my eyes.

'You know Heath is resilient, Cathy. Before your father, God rest his soul, brought Heath home, the young lad had been surviving on his own on the streets already for several years. Don't you be worrying that he can't take care of himself. Our boy is a survivor.'

I loved that she called him that. Nelly genuinely loved Heath. But then again, Nelly loved every stray that wandered into our life from the people and animal kingdom!

I ate a few more mouthfuls of her excellent scrambled eggs before talking about Heath again. God, I was even boring myself these days with my fixation!

'I've gone over it in my head a thousand times, Nelly,' I said. 'Why did he just leave like that? Do you think he heard our discussion… when I said I wasn't sure about him, our future, you know, as a couple?'

Nelly took a deep breath. 'He might have, my love. But then why run, why not confront you then and there?'

'Maybe he was too hurt. I didn't mean he wasn't good enough for me or that I didn't want him to be part of my life,' I said, aware I was rambling with self-justifications. 'I just meant that he and I are all we've ever known. How can we be sure that what we feel is real and not dependence? And how do we know if it's enough to last the distance? How does anyone know?'

'Oh, I knew with my husband, Albie. I knew the moment I met him he was the one… God, I was a fool for that man,' Nelly said, and smiled.

'Exactly,' I agreed with Nelly and finished my toast. 'Was he mad about you?'

'Oh he was, he proposed every day, but I didn't accept him until we'd been going out for six months. My parents thought that was too soon!'

I smiled and sighed. 'How romantic. I'm mad about Heath but is that even healthy at our age? Should I be doing what everyone says and be going out with other people while we're young and not settling just because he's there? And then some people think it's creepy because we're related but we're not related, we just grew up in the same house together.'

'I don't know Cathy,' Nelly said. 'People are full of good advice when their heart is not at stake. As for Heath, I've always had a soft spot for that young man. He's got goodness in him but this was never a happy home for him – Hindley made him feel unwelcome from day one and he never really developed a relationship with your dear mother. If you and your father weren't here, I firmly believe Heath would have left years ago, maybe tried to seek out his people.'

'Why leave now when it is pretty much just you and me here? The two people who genuinely love him.' As I asked the question I heard a car horn out the front. I drained my glass of juice and rose.

'That's Tilly. Got to go, thanks for breakfast, Nelly.' I placed a kiss on her cheek again and felt her watching me with concern as I grabbed my school bag and headed to the front door.

Nelly was the only relative alive now who felt any genuine concern for me. Although maybe Hindley would shed a tear if I was gone, maybe not. Did Heath still care for me? Enough already, that's it. I'm not thinking about him at all today. Not one thought.

*****

My best friend, Tilly, beeped the horn of her car as she idled in the driveway outside. I slid into the front seat and greeted her. She looked cute in a pale blue twin set; I had put little thought into my jeans and hippie top. I had to get a grip soon. I couldn't let Heath completely ruin my last year of school.

'Oh my God, your brother is gorgeous,' she exclaimed, after giving me an air kiss. 'I could stare into those dark eyes all day and run my hands...'

I cut her off. 'Ugh, stop. Hindley? Really? When did you see him?'

'On the way to pick you up. He passed me about fifteen minutes ago. Gave me this wave and a big smile... gorgeous. Is he seeing anyone?'

'You mean since you last asked two days ago?' I smirked at her. 'There are about five girlfriends who think they are the only one at the moment, so don't go there unless you want to be number six. Besides, you're better than that.'

'Hmm am I? We could be sisters, officially like sisters legally, wouldn't that be cool?' Tilly exclaimed, cruising down our long driveway and turning out onto the road.'

'We are sisters. Besides, it will only end in tears and then you'll hate me because you hate him and—'

'Fine, I get the picture,' Tilly cut me off. 'So you don't think he'd go to the formal dance with me if I asked him?'

I turned to look at her in horror, and she laughed.

'I'm just kidding, lighten up,' she said. 'Save your foul mood for the first-period history with Mr Mead.'

I groaned. 'Red,' I said.

'Blue,' Tilly answered, and we shook hands. We always took a running bet on what coloured plaid shorts he would wear each day… he had an impressive collection. The winner buys cola at lunch time.

'I'll have a diet cola when I win,' she said, getting her order in early.

I gave her another one of my smirks. At this rate, I'd have none left by the end of the day.

*****

I could feel someone staring at me and I looked up from writing in my notepad to find Isabella Linton watching me from across the school café. She raised her fingers in a feeble wave and smiled like she'd been sprung. Isabella was a year younger and in the grade below. She looked so much like her brother Edgar… white-blonde hair, pale skin and those suck-you-in green eyes. Just when I thought she was going to come over, Tilly and Jason dropped down in front of me and blocked my view.

'Your cola,' Tilly said, pushing it towards me.

'Long live red shorts,' I said, 'thanks.'

'Something going on between you and Isabella?' Jason asked, glancing over his shoulder and giving her one of his knockout smiles. 'That would be hot seeing you two together.'

'Eww, no.' I looked at him and shook my head. 'Guys, honestly.'

'She's something else,' he exhaled. 'You could officially

introduce us. We'd be beautiful together… me with my velvet dark skin, Isabella with that milky white look, imagine the babies we'd produce,' he said.

'You really are strange, Jace,' Tilly said, tucking into her sandwich. Besides, I thought you were into Cathy.'

Jason looked embarrassed, which was kind of new for him.

Tilly shrugged. 'Just keeping it real. Didn't you want to ask her to the formal?'

'Did you, Jace?' I asked, and smiled, teasing him by going all girly and pushing a strand of hair back behind my ear. I looked up at him coquettishly. 'That's so sweet and romantic, and you're so handsome and strong.'

'You two suck,' he said, trying not to smile as he focussed on unwrapping his burger to the sound of our laughter.

What was there not to like about Jace? I just never looked at him like boyfriend potential because that guy I wasn't going to mention was always in my line of direct vision. I touched his arm and gave Jace a sincere smile because I was super flattered. Besides, I would never say 'yes' to Jace because Tilly was in love with him. She wouldn't admit it, but she had turned down three offers to go to the dance in the hope they'd go together even as friends like they did last time. She was right under his nose and he couldn't see her.

'Cathy can introduce you to Isabella, can't you?' she asked me. 'Ask her to the dance, Jace.' Tilly was her own worst enemy.

'Sure, she's lovely, but she's probably got a date already,' I offered. 'Tilly would have three if she accepted any of them.'

She grimaced at me, but Jace turned to look at her. A woman taken was always more interesting than a wallflower.

'Well if I get rejected, we can go together, can't we Til?' he asked.

Kill me now, just go together already.

'It's a standby date,' she agreed, and they bumped hands.

'Okay, introduce away, thanks,' he said to me. 'Strange family those Lintons. Remember her brother when he was a senior last year? Nice guy, just stand-offish. He and his friends were like the super-rich brats that never got dirty, and spent their time playing the stock exchange and sailing on weekends in yachts.'

I laughed. 'Get real, that's not them. But they were pretty sophisticated,' I agreed. 'At least they weren't the bad boys, like Heath's friends.'

Jace nodded. 'All that leather and snarling. They scared the hell out of me.'

Tilly stopped dreaming and joined in. 'Edgar Linton is gorgeous,' she sighed.

'You think everyone is gorgeous,' I reminded her.

'Including me,' Jace said.

'Especially you,' she agreed, and ribbed him.

'Why haven't you two ever hitched up?' I asked, trying to push the topic.

'Too much perfection,' Jace said.

Tilly agreed. 'It wouldn't be fair to not share it around.'

I rolled my eyes at the pair of them. My phone buzzed and I looked down, ever hopeful of a message from the guy that I wasn't going to think about all day. It was from Edgar.

'Ah speak of the devil,' I said and looked up. 'A message from Edgar.'

'How do you have his number? I didn't know you two were like a thing,' Tilly said, looking at me like I had conspired to keep the most important news of the day away from her.

'We're not a thing,' I said. 'I have his number because we had to go to a work function with our parents once and we fundraised for the prize. We worked on it together for weeks… it was a few years ago. He messaged me last night when he saw I was awake, wanted to catch up.' I shrugged, trying to make it all sound casual.

'Seriously? Is he not with Charlotte anymore?' Tilly asked.

'Charlotte, now she was something,' Jace continued. 'One glam ma'am.'

'I saw Charlotte the other day,' Tilly said. 'She was walking along the main street with some of her friends, looking like a catalogue. She's studying drama… I always thought she was a drama queen.'

I skimmed the message from Edgar while Jace and Tilly talked.

'Hey Cathy, great to connect last night. I've got to drop some bottles off at your business this pm. Will you be there? Be great to see you. E'

He wants to see me. Why? Don't get excited, he might just want to whine about what Hindley is doing with our joint company. We'd be up the creek if the Lintons want to pull out of business with us, I hope Hindley remembers that.

I messaged back. *'Sounds great, E. See you there about 4?'*

He sent back one word, '*Then*'.

Things suddenly felt a little brighter and lighter. Wish I'd worn something better today.

Chapter 4 – The deal is done

Heath

Make my day, it's a done deal, the ink is drying and call me boss. I catch my reflection in the glass office windows; it's kind of weird seeing myself in a suit but I'm liking it. I wonder what Cathy would think. I tower over the other two guys who I just bought the business from; we shake hands and that's it – I am now officially in the blood business. I've just got to work out who I can trust and who I can't amongst this new team. And now I can put the next part of my plan into action… it involves doing business with the Linton family and pushing Hindley out of our family business. Time to ring Edgar Linton. He has only just stepped up to run the business with his dad – but he knows me well enough to get me my foot in the door and talk about a future collaboration. This will seriously piss off Hindley. Can't wait. Well, no time like the present. I looked up the Linton Mortuary number and rang it.

'No condolences necessary,' I told the receptionist. 'I was just hoping to speak to Edgar.' She laughed… probably refreshing for her to not be always sympathetic. She took my name and put me through. He sounded surprised and wary, can't blame him. We've met about half a dozen times in eleven years, so we're hardly besties. I told him about my new gig and he congratulated me and agreed to a meeting. We set a time for next week, he was interested in coming to my premises – only natural he'd want to tour a blood bank, a private blood bank where storing blood and selling blood at a good price is what we're all about. Lucky he hadn't gone through the Conversion yet or the pull might be too strong.

I had work to do now; I was going to present him with a partnership plan. It's probably his very own first deal he can present to his business board that promises a better future for both the Earnshaws and Lintons. Yeah, I'm getting ahead of myself but if Cathy comes on board too, this could be the next generation. After the Conversion, then we'll all benefit from it.

I'm almost ready to return to Cathy.

God, I miss her every moment of every day, it's like I'd left half of me behind when I left The Moors. I've been back two days, lying low which makes it worse, it's like I can sense her and smell her sweet fragrance in the wind. Last night I stood outside in the shadows, I heard her call out my name and I wanted so much just to rush upstairs and hold her. It took every fibre in my body not to move but I have to do this right. Every day of the past year I've thought about the vultures circling her, waiting to move in on her while I'm away if they haven't already. She's beautiful and single.

Still, I don't regret what I've done, it's for the best. You know the old saying, 'If you love someone set them free, and they'll come back if they are yours' or some crap like that. Well, that better not be shite, because I've just lived through the most painful year of my life setting Cathy free while I bettered myself, and now I'm going to test the theory and see if she comes back to me, willingly.

I had a plan to return to her as the man she deserves. Successful, in charge, and I have another agenda too. To piss off that nob of a brother of hers, Hindley, and bring him to his knees. He worried that a new son and heir had come into the house all those years ago, well you were right to worry, bro, the prodigal son has returned and he is going to wipe you out. All the kindness and the lessons your father taught me, all the business acumen he shared, I've sucked that up while you were swaggering around like you own the place because one day you would, but I'm going to use it all against you. Thanks, Dad.

Soon my girl, Cathy, and I will work happily with the Lintons, respecting their expertise while you, Hindley, struggle to keep afloat.

I can't breathe for thinking about the reunion we'll have. Her face will be the first thing I see of a morning and the last thing I see at night. Cathy and Heath, how it is meant to be.

*****

The lawyer, Miles Gailbraith, returns and hands me a copy of the papers. 'Congratulations,' he says, and we shake hands.

I studied him; he'd be nearing retirement age any day now; a lot of knowledge locked up in that head. He reminds me of Dad a bit… pressed, neat, expensive but kindly look.

'Well your deal might be one of the last I do,' he said and emptied his glass.

'Why's that?' I asked. 'Are you retiring?'

'That's the line,' Miles said, with a sigh. 'I'm being shown the door. Young blood making its way up the ladder and we oldies aren't too fashionable for the firm anymore.'

I scoffed. Sounds like something Hindley would do.

'Do you want to retire?' I asked.

'No. I love my work, always have. I'd be happy with a couple of days a week work, just to stay fresh, and a few days on the golf course.'

I smiled. 'I was hoping you'd say that. Any chance you'd consider working those few days with me, here, Miles? I've got some business deals coming up that would fit you perfectly and I need a man who knows all the legal traps so I have my back covered.'

And that's how I put on my very first employee. Yeah, I'm liking this business stuff.

I'm coming home to you, Cathy, and now I deserve you. You'll see.

Chapter 5 – Dress to impress

Catherine

'You can't wear that if you are meeting Linton after school,' Tilly said, looking me up and down as if I had just walked out of a second-store and thrown on something totally uncoordinated! That's what I love about Tilly, she'll always give it to me straight.

She was right. If I'd known that I was going to see Edgar – the same Edgar who always looked beautiful and always wore a suit when working, and linen casuals when not – then hippy pattern and jeans didn't cut it.

'This calls for drastic action,' she said. Pushing away her lunch wrapping.

'It does?' I asked.

'It does?' Jace asked, tuning into the conversation late.

Tilly held up her hand to him. 'This is a girl fashion crisis, Jace. And since you are neither a girl nor gay with an inner fashion radar, you're out of this one.'

'Phew, that's a relief because I had nothing,' he said, with another glance over his shoulder. Isabella Linton was still sitting there with some friends. He smiled at her and she smiled sweetly at him and looked away.

He turned back to find us watching. 'That's promising, isn't it?'

'Very,' I said and looked at Tilly. 'Back to ground zero. What shall I do about this wardrobe, I don't have time to go home?'

She nodded. 'Leave it with me. I need dress size and shoe size,' she said, and I supplied them. 'Skinny bitch,' she replied. And with that, she grabbed her phone and began tapping away.

'Right,' she said, looking up. 'It took him long enough.'

'Who?' I said, looking around, expecting to see someone.

'Edgar Linton!' Tilly exclaimed. 'He used to look at you all the time, don't know why he just didn't come up and talk with you. Every girl in his year and the years below were gagging to talk with him.

I frowned. 'Nuh, you're dreaming. Edgar Linton never looked at me.'

'Cathy, you wouldn't have noticed it he did. Let's not kid ourselves, you've been blinkered,' she said. 'Me, well I've got a radar for this sort of thing.'

She looked around the school café. 'See that guy by the window, Eric, he's made for Sally and she's made for Eric. Eric is interested in her but frankly would prefer Karran, and Taylor's keen on me but frankly, he's got to work for that.'

I laughed and shook my head. 'So complex.'

'Hell yeah,' Jace butted in. 'Like you're going to put it out there if it is not coming back. You've had Heath on tap for years, the rest of us have got to sift and sort through the pack.'

'So romantic,' I said.

Tilly's phone pinged with a message; she glanced at the screen.

'You are sorted, Ms Earnshaw. After the last class, Sandy, my cousin, will meet us in the car park with dress and shoe options. She's on maternity leave and has a wardrobe of chic and corporate fashions. She's your size and height, and she owes me.'

I clapped my hands together. 'Tilly, I love you,' I said, and she smiled.

'I am loveable,' she agreed. With that, the bell rang for the last three lessons of the day, and Isabella Linton began walking away.

I grabbed Jace's arm. 'Hang on a sec,' I said. 'I'll introduce you to Isabella when she passes.'

I knew then he was in love; he froze in fear and anticipation. I had to reach over and close his jaw. As she neared, I smiled and asked her how she was.

'I'm good, Catherine, and you?' she asked. She was so like Edgar. Gentle, beautiful, and sincere. She looked at me like I was the only person in the room and she was waiting with great anticipation for my answer. What a skill – must come from being raised in a business where you ask people all the time how they are.

'I'm well, I feel like I haven't seen you in forever. Have you met my friends, Tilly and Jason?'

She said hello and Jason rose and shook her hand. Nice touch. He lingered on releasing his hand, she smiled shyly and looked away. My job is done here, God, I'm good.

So back to me; in two hours, I'd be meeting with Isabella's brother. Edgar Linton. The guy who has been connected to my family forever and who barely gave me a second glance at school, despite what Tilly said. But then I pulled myself back down to earth. Let's not get too excited, he might just want to meet with me to tell me that Hindley's a pain in the butt and that he's systematically destroying the business. Sigh. At least I'll be well dressed for that.

*****

I realised in my last class, English studies, that I hadn't thought of Heath for close to ninety minutes; this was big, really big. If I could just stop thinking of him at night, that'd be brilliant. It was thanks to Edgar.

I tuned back into the lesson. We were studying great poets and if Edgar hadn't thrown me a lifeline – something to distract me from my current missing Heath agony – I would wallow in the drama as Mr Wall read aloud: "*How do I love thee? Let me count the ways. I love thee to the depth and breadth and height my soul can reach.*" Thank you, Elizabeth Barrett Browning, those words speak to my soul. Heath, that was you last week buddy, I loved you to the moon and back, but now anger is taking over and you've dropped me for an entire year so you are so out.

No sooner had I uttered these brave thoughts, and I was

overwhelmed with guilt and missing Heath. I didn't mean what I said. I love him. I hope he is okay; I pray he is okay.

Heath is more myself than I am.

He gets me, I get him. But what if he never comes back?

Chapter 6 – The firm

Catherine

'Perfect,' Tilly said, 'you look gorgeous. My cousin is a genius.' She stood back, pulling and plucking at me, making sure everything was tucked in or pushed out.

It was a beautiful white dress, super feminine, and I wore silver slippers and let my dark hair out. I felt like I was a virgin on a debut night! Too much? Yeah, probably.

I could only see extracts of myself reflected in the small school toilet mirrors, but hey, it was a big improvement on the jeans and hippie shirt.

'Thank you, Tilly, I owe you. It'd be funny if he didn't show after all this or if he's still seeing Charlotte and just wanted me to help with some work type thing.'

'It would be so not funny,' she said and gave me a wry look.

'You're right, so not funny. Righto, let's get out of here. You don't have to drop me at the firm,' I said, which is what I called our winery business.

'Of course I will, it's on my way,' she said.

'It's five k's out of town!'

'Yeah, well I feel like a drive.' She tugged at her hair, released the clip and brushed it out. Tilly dabbed on some powder and light lipstick. Noticing me noticing her, she shrugged.

'I might meet someone gorgeous in the car park.'

'Good thinking.' *Not. And especially not Hindley.*

I packed up my hippie reject gear and when Tilly was done, we exited the building and headed towards the school car park. She unlocked the car doors, we threw our bags in the back seat and slipped into the front.

'You want to come in and say hi to Hindley?' I asked with dread. I owed her after all.

'Nuh, I think I'll take your advice. I am a girl who likes to be the one and only.'

'You're worth it,' I agreed, and she giggled like I was telling her something she didn't know. 'Come in any way, meet Edgar officially.'

'Okay, thanks,' she said, and brightened. 'Why not?'

'You can take home a nice bottle of wine for your folks,' I suggested. 'Keeps me in their good books which isn't a bad thing.'

As we drove out of the village, Tilly glanced over at me. 'I bet Edgar likes girly girls. You know the types who are feminine and sweet, no tatts or strange waxing patterns,' Tilly said.

'Eww,' I said, trying not to think about that last statement. 'Why do you think that?' I asked.

'Look at his mum and sister, look at Charlotte. All glamorous and feminine,' she gave me a quick smile before returning her eyes to the road. 'You'll fit right in.'

I groaned. 'Making too much of this. He's just an old family friend and he's in the 'hood and wants to say hi. Probably going to tell me how much his family is missing Dad being in charge.'

Our winery came into site and it made me miss Dad and Mum even more; in the past, they were always there. Dad would walk the grounds, behind the scenes he'd be hands-on in every aspect of the business – he knew every staff member's name and their spouse's name and their kids' names. The annual staff family Christmas parties were legendary and generous. This was his lifeblood. Mum also was part of the fabric here. She oversaw the restaurant and café, playing the host. She was charming and social, everything I couldn't be bothered with. People exhausted me, but she was an extrovert and loved it.

'It's looking beautiful,' Tilly said as the afternoon light reflected on the green vines.

'Thanks,' I said, like I was responsible. 'It's a good season supposedly.' I shrugged. I had little to do with the business except during school breaks, but I would step up when I finished school this year.

That reminded me to offer Tilly work. 'Even though Mum and Dad are gone, there's still holiday work there if we want it.'

'Hell yeah,' Tilly said. 'Dad might have bought me this car, but my allowance is still shit. Besides, it's kind of fun working in the café.'

Tilly was such a flirt. I knew exactly what kind of fun she was talking about.

As we drew closer, the enormity of the business blew me away. It was the biggest winery in West Yorkshire, by far – acres and acres of our scraggly trees in straight lines up the rise as far as the eye could see before they disappeared over the edge. Behind it was an impressive glass building, the restaurant and café, which was hugely popular too, and a car park that regularly overflowed with cars and tourist buses. Who didn't like a glass of Chardy with their smashed avo and moors view?

Then two floors below, out of the public eye, cool and artificially lit, was the office for our other business – bottling the blood supplied from the Linton Mortuary for the other residents of The Moors, residents like me. We call it blood wine and we also look after distributing it to the clients on our database. Yep, something for everyone.

Tilly pulled up in the car park closest to the office entrance. The car park was pretty empty now… the café and restaurant had closed, wine tastings were done for the day but you could still buy bottled wine over the counter.

In the car park nearby was my brother Hindley's car, it was black, fast and sporty, of course. Beside it was Edgar's car – a very sophisticated white Audi two-door sporty looking… whatever, it was perfect and I could see myself in that. The happy thought also hit me that Edgar couldn't fit a lot of empty wine bottles in there, so maybe he wasn't really here to do a delivery of refillables. Maybe he was here to deal with some small business matter with Heath on the pretence of catching up with me! He made the meeting after school time. Had he broken up with Charlotte?

Maybe we had both been dumped. Or just maybe this was meant to be.

*****

We walked down the hallways of the offices and I greeted people as we went through. So many old friends and faces and each wanting to share a kind word and to see how I was travelling since Dad and Mum had passed on. It was easier to say that than to say they had died. It sounded so infinitely final.

Nearly everyone knew Tilly from our summer stints working here and she was warmly greeted. We made our way to the café and grabbed a cola each from the fridge. I couldn't take Tilly through to the other part of the business, so we loitered with intent. Hindley's assistant – who used to be Dad's – would tell him and Edgar we were here.

After about ten minutes, I saw Hindley and Edgar walking towards us. Oh my God, Edgar really was something. How had I not seen that before? Probably because he was with Charlotte and I was with Heath. He caught my eye and smiled this knockout smile. Kill me now. I smiled back and felt Tilly nudged me.

'I told you he likes you,' she said. They came to the café entrance and stopped just inside the door to finish their discussion before joining us. Blood business that they couldn't discuss in front of Tilly.

I looked at Hindley for the first time and gasped.

'What's wrong?' Tilly snapped to look at me.

I stumbled to come up with an excuse. 'It's okay, I thought I'd lost my phone… I couldn't live without it.'

'Who could?' she agreed, quickly glancing in her bag to check her own was there.

I couldn't believe it; I knew the moment I saw Hindley he had converted.

Chapter 7 – The Conversion

Catherine

To say it pissed me off was a super, major, global-sized understatement. Hindley had undergone the Conversion and not shared it with me. His eyes were emerald green, bright as could be. Now I understand why Tilly said he looked gorgeous when he passed by her this morning; he was vampirised! His skin was glowing, eyes bright, every feature drew you in and he looked, well, beautiful.

I can't believe he would convert, just like that. It's supposed to be a coming-of-age celebration. Everything about our lives was a journey of small milestones, planned out according to our culture – an ancient culture – that culminated in the Conversion, and Hindley had just pissed on it! How very Hindley.

We were told stories of our ancestors when we were children. It scared most kids stiff hearing of vampires and ghouls, but we were told of a noble, secret order that we came from and that our descendants would come from. We didn't hunt wild beasts or humans like in the movies and TV shows, although they did in past generations. But everyone's descendants did barbaric things in past generations, we just happened to be really good at it!

At sixteen, when we were old enough to understand and to consider our future, we underwent an Acceptance Ceremony. Heath did it too, Dad wanted us all to be equal. That's when we were told the full story of the Conversion – we knew a 'kiddy' version that you grow up with; to other kids, it was just a fairy tale, a fantasy. But at sixteen, we learnt that we have a choice to go through the Conversion ceremony and be immortal or to live out our normal life. We are not Dhampyre, that's truly frowned upon – the union of a vampire with a human. If you convert, you have to partner with someone from our culture, and if you choose not to convert and stay human, then your partner must be human.

They conducted the Conversion ceremonies on partial, penumbral or total eclipse dates. The stronger the eclipse, the easier your Conversion. We all wanted a blood moon – the deep coppery red colour of the moon made for a magic night and great photos once you were through the Conversion. It must have been painful for Hindley to have done it with no eclipse at all.

It was a big thing to choose not to convert given our history, but it wasn't shameful. Some people wanted to experience all that a normal life offered, while others wanted the long life of a vampire with extraordinary health, the opportunity to see in new decades and centuries, to see, hear, feel and touch things with extraordinary sensory powers. And to be amongst the beautiful set, especially when you moved in the European circles and the annual ball calendar.

And there were milestones. You could convert at 21 years of age; it was called Youth Dew. You stayed that age forever, and that had its own complications because it meant you had to seriously consider if you wanted to have kids and plan for that by freezing eggs and other stuff. Plus, you had to keep moving on once your kids become your age, or start flatting together like friends – you couldn't have kids your own age calling you mum and dad. But if you were sure you didn't want to have kids, then Youth Dew was a good option.

The next official ceremony phase was called Vie Mature. It meant mature life, and we undertook it at thirty years of age. By then you could have your family and you were at an age where you could blend into the community for decades to come. Edgar's parents chose Vie Mature and they were greying their hair a little to look late forties. Eventually, they will move on and leave the business to Edgar and Isabella to run while they begin a new life elsewhere at thirty again. It's exciting and glamorous and full of opportunity.

Sometimes though, it didn't go as planned and you just had to have the Conversion or you missed the opportunity because of illness or accident, and sometimes it was too late. This was a tragedy for our culture. I guess in that instance it was a bit like normal mortal life in some respects. So you could do Impulsion, if you needed to any time that the moon was right, at any age between 21 and 30. It just didn't have the ceremony aspect or the cultural celebration that the other two milestones did. It was kind of like having a huge 24th birthday party when 18 and 21 is the done thing.

I was ninety-five per cent positive I was going to convert; in all honesty, the only reason I was not one hundred per cent was because of Heath – if he didn't convert then how would we spend a life together? I'd have to rethink everything, our future, my plans, and be sure that I could make that sacrifice. I wasn't sure if I'd do Youth Dew or Vie Mature, the jury was still out on that one, but there was no rush to make that decision. I guess I worried if I converted too young what would happen with my friendships. How long would I be able to hang out with Tilly and Jace if I'm looking 21 and they're looking 45! So much to think of and consider.

Our non-Sanguineous Immortalis friends' parties celebrated 21st or 30th birthdays so we invited them to the same, but to those of our friends who were part of our culture, they knew they were Conversion balls. I was a little scared about the process but I'd prepare for that later if I went that way; it was still four years away for me at least!

But Hindley had just done it; no discussion, no celebration, nothing. He saw me staring at him and gave me a wink. He could be so charming. I gave him a look back that hopefully said: "that won't get you off the hook, big brother, you just wait!"

Hindley and Edgar finished their discussion and entered the café where we were waiting.

'Well don't you look, lovely, little Sis,' he said and kissed me on the cheek.

'As do you, bro,' I said, narrowing my eyes at him. He gave me a cheeky grin. His eyes were amazing, so beautiful. He turned to Tilly and kissed her on the cheek as well, holding her hand a little longer than necessary. I thought she was going to faint.

'You do look lovely, Cathy,' Edgar said. He didn't attempt the kiss on the cheek… damn him.

'Thank you,' I said, because truly that was all that I could manage without making myself look like a bigger idiot standing there swooning. I turned to Tilly and introduced them.

'Tilly, this is Edgar Linton – Edgar, my best friend, Matilda McCarthy.'

'I remember you from school,' Edgar said, shaking Tilly's hand.

'Everyone calls me Tilly,' she said, blushing. Really we were both hopeless.

'I'd love to stay and chat,' Hindley said, again being charming – what the…? 'But,' he continued, 'I've got to get back to work. Thanks for coming by, Edgar, good talk,' he said, with a handshake. 'Ladies,' he said with a small bow. Yeah, maybe Conversion suited him. And with that, he disappeared through the café door, back to the basement no doubt. We'd talk later, Hindley, you're not getting off that lightly.

I remembered I promised Tilly a bottle of wine for her folks and got up to grab one of the more expensive bottles from the café cellar and one for Edgar, too. He was still drinking grape wine; his parents, however, were a different story and we didn't keep blood wine – as it was called – in the public areas, naturally.

'Oh wow, thank you,' Tilly said, 'I'm sure Mum and Dad will enjoy it.'

Edgar thanked me and looked at the label. 'Good grapes, a good year,' he said, 'thank you.'

'My pleasure,' I told them.

'Well, I'd best get going,' Tilly said, realising two is company, three is cramping my style and reducing the opportunity for gossip tomorrow at school.

'You won't stay and finish your cola?' Edgar asked. So charming.

'I've got a deadline on an assignment, but thanks. Cathy would have already done it I imagine,' she said, with a look to me and a smile.

'Ah, that old thing, almost done. I'll walk you out,' I offered. But she was up and telling Edgar how lovely it was to officially meet him, and waving bye to me before I had the chance.

I turned to Edgar, his deep blue eyes were watching me. They would be stunning when he converted – I wondered if they would go lighter blue or darker blue. I sat back down and he grabbed a juice from the fridge, offering me another. I declined, and he joined me at a table.

'It's been ages since I've seen you,' he said.

'Since we organised that charity prize,' I said, reminding him.

He laughed. 'I remember that event… you were ruthless getting those prizes. I wouldn't be game not to give you a donation.'

I laughed at the memory. 'I was on a mission,' I said, defending myself.

'Nothing wrong with that; I like a girl with direction,' he said, teasing me.

He was so hot. We had an awkward minute of silence which felt like a year, then we both spoke at once.

'How's Charl—'

'I heard from—'

'Please, you first,' he said, being a gentleman. God, he's gorgeous, did I mention that?

'How's Charlotte?' I asked, fishing. I hope that wasn't too obvious. Yeah, it was.

He sat back in the chair and breathed out. 'She's enjoying her drama studies, I believe. We've gone separate ways.'

'Oh, I'm sorry,' I said, doing my best to fake surprise and sincerity – so not sorry. See ya Charlotte.

'It was good when it was good, but you know, we had little in common and what little we had we'd grown out of. I'm sure she'll be happier with someone else,' he said.

So will you, Edgar, like with me! I thought. I'm glad he didn't bag her, that would have been tacky, although I wouldn't mind a little more detail on how unsuited they were and how she's not his type and how he'd like his girlfriend to have long dark hair and… I'm back, I got carried away then. I sipped my cola daintily, waiting for what he was going to say earlier before I interrupted him. It is so hard to wear white, you've got to be careful eating, drinking, breathing!

'So, Hindley's converted,' he said.

'I know,' I said, my eyes wide with surprise. 'Caught me by surprise.'

'You didn't know?'

'No. I don't know when he did it but it must have been recently… he hadn't converted when we spoke on the weekend. He didn't have a ceremony; I don't even know if he did the medical stuff, preserved… you know.' I didn't want to say sperm out loud. If I went with the Youth Dew choice, I'd be preserving my eggs just in case I changed my mind and wanted to have kids later, after all. Converting takes away your natural chance of conceiving, it's one of the few downsides.

He cleared his throat and looked up at me. 'I know it's a personal question, but do you think you will when the time comes… you know, undertake the Conversion?'

I nodded. 'I'm planning to. Will you?'

'Of course. I've always known I would,' he said, with cool confidence. So attractive.

I smiled. 'Well, you are pure-sang,' I reminded him. Edgar's family were one of the few families that were pure blood. Every generation of his descendants since time immemorial had chosen the Conversion. That's why he was a slightly paler colour than most of our culture, from the pure line.

'The same can't be said of my line.' I added.

'Nothing wrong with that,' he said graciously. 'Love is love. If you fall in love and someone will convert for you, well that's pretty powerful. The same goes if they don't convert for love. I'm guessing that's your parent's story?'

I nodded. 'Mum didn't want to convert. She offered to break up with Dad and let him find a love who would, but he wouldn't hear of it.'

‘Does it make you angry now that they’ve gone… that they chose to die like all Saps?’

I swallowed my emotions while I prepared to answer.

‘Sorry,’ Edgar cut in, ‘I don’t want to upset you, we don’t have to talk about this,’ he said, with sensitivity. He moved his hand across the table and covered mine; it took my breath away for a moment and I forgot what he said.

I cleared my throat. ‘No, it’s fine. I like talking about them, it keeps them alive if that makes sense? But yeah, I’ve been through that phase, blaming their human frailty, blaming the other driver, blaming Mum for not converting, blaming everyone in the world… but, it is what it is,’ I said, and gave a little shrug. ‘Maybe that’s why Hindley rushed into it. He turned 21 four months ago, about the time they died so everything went on hold for a while.’

‘Maybe,’ Edgar said. ‘He might have just wanted to get it happening so he could focus on the business.’

I nodded, watching Edgar’s reaction and reading between the lines.

‘He’s making it very difficult, isn’t he?’ I asked.

Edgar nodded and held my gaze; I really couldn’t concentrate when he did that.

‘Well, business is business,’ he said, ‘but yeah, you might say he’s on a power trip. He’s changing our agreed rates which my folks and your dad reviewed every year, anyway. It’s not due for review for another eight months. But there’s no formal contract anymore… this arrangement we have has been in place for—’

‘Generations,’ I said.

'Generations,' he agreed. 'It's good to see you.'

'And you too.' I smiled, and I looked down at my hands, at the table, anywhere. How awkward, could I be any more pathetic?

He kept looking at me. 'I was wondering if you might want to go out on Saturday night, maybe a movie or there's a good band playing at the Grand Hotel if you're into live bands.'

My heart rate went up... I could hear it beating fast. Thank God we weren't converted or he'd hear it too, how embarrassing.

But Saturday, no! I stumbled over my words. 'I can't on—'

He cut me off. 'No, that's fine, it was just a thought, it's been good to see you anyway.'

'No,' I interrupted him, 'I'd love to go out, thank you.'

He smiled, as pleased as me... well, maybe I was more excited than he was.

'It's just that Saturday is the school dance – the Solstice Dance.'

'Ah, of course, I should have remembered. I'm only one year out of school and I've forgotten already. Plus, Isabella has been talking about it all week – what to wear, do her shoes go with the dress, does her butt look big in ten different dresses!' He rolled his eyes and he rattled them off and I laughed at his impressions.

'Will you take me?' I asked. Non-school partners could escort us.

'Really?' he asked, and laughed.

I shrugged. 'You don't have to go back to school if you don't want to, we could go out another time.'

'No, it would be my pleasure to escort you,' he said and smiled like he really wanted.

'Great,' I said, grinning. I was going to be walking in with Edgar Linton, the guy every girl wanted to take them to the dance. 'Besides,' I reminded him, 'it will be worth it just to see Mr Mead swap his shorts for long pants.'

Edgar groaned at the memory. 'Speaking of which, is there a theme? Do I have to wear something bizarre?' he asked.

'The theme is glamorous. So black-tie?'

'That I can do,' he said.

I bet you can Edgar Linton. OMG now I have to rethink my entire outfit and it's only two days away. This calls for drastic action – Tilly again.

'Well, text me the time and I'll pick you up,' he said, rising. 'I'd best be going and let you catch up with Hindley or whoever you were meeting.'

'I'd better,' I agreed, knowing I was catching up with absolutely no one; I came here to meet Edgar, but I didn't want to appear that keen.

'See you Saturday,' he said, and took my hand, then released it just as quickly.

'Saturday,' I said, and walked him to the door.

'Oh, I heard from your adopted brother,' Edgar said.

'Heath? You heard from Heath?' I said, stopping in my tracks.

Edgar nodded.

'But where is he? He's been gone for over a year. He's not here, is he?' I peppered him with questions, forgetting my awe for Edgar. I'm sure I did not impress him with my over-enthusiastic Heath interest.

'He's back in town. He's just bought a business and wants to talk with me about it.'

'He's back?' I choked on the words. Edgar nodded and gave me a wave as he departed through the door.

And with those two words, I was back in Heath-land.

Chapter 8 – A night-time visit

Catherine

Nelly and I had just finished having dinner; Hindley wouldn't be joining us for meals anymore – he'd just be helping himself to the best-bottled blood wine he could get his hands on at work, and the grape wines to no doubt. Whatever. It was a good night to be inside – chilly, windy and dark… the moon buried in clouds.

After I asked after Nelly's day and heard about how the annual *Literary Walk Along the Moors* festival was coming along – she helped every year – I was relieved when she asked after my day so I could fill her in and rage about the Heath news for the rest of the meal. I suspect over the years she's learnt to tune out when Hindley and I were having our self-indulgent rants.

Now, the meal finished, as Nelly and I sat over a cup of tea, I told her about Edgar. I swear her eyes misted up… she always had a soft spot for the Linton family. Nelly worked there for a while but left after Linton was born and his parents went through the Conversion. She came to work for my folks and never left. It's not that the Lintons could not control themselves having Saps in the house and the smell of blood – their children were human and the supply of blood wine today was so superior no one went hungry in any price range. It's just easier to have adults in the same house with the same culture. So Nelly came to us, thank goodness. She was all I had now, and I loved her like a grandmother. Nelly wasn't one of us, but she shared our culture. She and her husband had once chosen not to convert and they had forty years together before illness took him. He was our gardener for most of those years. Nelly said they never regretted it, but I know she is lonely sometimes.

'You will be so beautiful together you two young people. I can't wait to see you both happy,' she said, taking a lace white handkerchief from her breast pocket and dabbing her eyes.

I took her hand. 'You softie,' I teased her, and she laughed.

'He's a lovely boy, and Isabella, such a sweet girl, too. I can't think of anyone else who I'd rather see you with. Now about a dress for this dance…'

'I know. There goes Saturday, I'll be shopping.' I had to keep my spending in order though, Tilly couldn't afford the things I could and I didn't want to show off or make her feel bad. Besides, it's only one night and only one dress… that has to look brilliant.

'Something glamorous and sophisticated, well the theme is glamorous, isn't it?' Nelly asked.

A loud knock at the door cut my answer short. I glanced at the clock; it was 7.30pm. A bit early for Hindley's party crowd and like they ever knocked.

'I'll get it,' I said, and rose, calling over my shoulder, 'it's probably one of Hindley's friends whose lost the way for tonight's hang out.'

I opened the front door and Heath stood there. In the doorway, silhouetted by the dark sky.

I can't remember what I did, but I felt myself stumble back a step or two and gasp. Nelly, on hearing me, rushed from the kitchen.

'Cathy!' and then she saw Heath.

'Heath,' she cried, 'oh my boy, we thought we'd lost you for good.' She raced forward towards him and he grabbed her in an embrace, never taking his eyes off me.

'Nelly, I've missed you,' he said.

Oh my, he looked so good. We just stared at each other. It was like he had sucked all the oxygen out of the room – I stood there mouth agape, hand on my heart and drank him in. He was different; confident, stylish. I don't know I couldn't put my finger on it, but he looked like a man. He was wearing jeans, a white T-shirt and a black jacket like he had just stepped out of a men's catalogue. His brown eyes were clear and watching me, but he hadn't gone through the Conversion; he was clean-shaven and his dark hair cut short – so sexy.

'Cathy,' he said.

Nelly stood back. 'Well, I'm going to leave you both to catch up. Welcome home, Heath. Good night then, I'll see you in the morning, Cathy.'

'Good night, Nelly,' Heath said, still watching me.

'Good night, Nelly, thank you for dinner,' I said, staring

at Heath. He turned and closed the front door behind him, and then returned his gaze to me.

He was home. He was different, and I was not sure my heart could handle it.

*****

Heath

On the nights when I lay alone thinking about Cathy, I had pictured our reunion in my head a thousand times; watching it unfold in slow motion, with me being the hero, Cathy clutching me like she couldn't breathe without me. She would see me and run towards me, throwing her arms around me in a tight embrace. She would cry, I would hold her until she begged to pull away.

It wasn't happening. She stared at me; that soon changed and she glared at me.

'Cathy,' I said, and stepped towards her. She moved back and put her hands up in front of her.

'Don't come a step closer, Heath.' Her eyes filled with tears and my heart ached, this was not how it was supposed to go down.

'I've missed you so—'

'Not enough,' she cut me off, anger flaring in her eyes. 'You have not missed me enough to spare me one thought in a year and four weeks!'

I stood to full height. Two could play at being angry.

'I have done nothing else but think of you from the

moment I left here until this moment. Everything…,' and I stressed the word, 'everything, that I have done for the past year has been for you. I wouldn't have left if it hadn't been for you.'

She crossed her arms across her chest and looked so gorgeous I wanted to clutch her in my arms.

'Well, I guess I should thank you,' she said smartly. 'Thank you, Heath, for the stress, and worry, and sleepless nights. Thanks for letting me think you were dead, or that you had left my family for good. Thanks for leaving my life after being in it every single day since I was six and just clearing out. Because I had already lost Mum and Dad, and then you, you who are my rock, just vanish.' She waved her hands in the air like it was unthinkable that I didn't get it.

Oh God, this was a mess.

'Let me explain—'

Cathy cut me off and stepped forward and around me, her hand reaching for the door handle. She was so close I couldn't help myself; I grabbed her and held her. At first, she sobbed and let me, and then she shoved me away with such unexpected force that I fell back a step before righting myself.

'Get away from me Heath, you left,' she cried. 'We're not Heath and Cathy anymore, we're nothing. Just leave.'

Rage ran through me, and the wind outside matched my anger. The door frame rattled, the window panes shook, and the wind roared down the fireplace.

I tried to stay calm. I narrowed my eyes at her and said in a low voice: 'I heard what you said to Nelly, that you wondered what else was out there and if I was good enough—'

'I never said that,' she cut me off. 'I never said you weren't good enough.'

'You may as well have. You wanted to get away from me and see who else might be better for you, play the field. So I gave you that chance,' I snapped back at her. 'I gave you space and went and made something of myself to come back to you better, to be someone you deserve. I've got a new business, I'm financially independent, I found my heritage—' I didn't get to finish. She stood close to me, her eyes staring me down.

'And during that entire time, you never thought to let me know you were okay, or to message me that you were just off doing your own thing and you'd see me soon? That would have done. I would have taken anything.' Her voice hitched, but she refused to give in to her tears or me.

I took a deep breath. 'Cathy, let me stay.'

'This is your family home,' she reminded me. 'You don't need me to invite you to stay, there's your bedroom.' She pointed to the hall behind the staircase. 'And you don't need me to tell you when you come and go, you've made that clear.'

This was so not going well.

'Can we get a drink, sit down and talk,' I said, with a nod to the kitchen.

'Help yourself to anything you want. I'm going to bed. I'm sure you remember where the kitchen is.'

I grabbed her hand. 'Cathy, don't do this.'

'Do what?' Her eyes flared, and she snatched her hand away from me.

'Leave us. Don't leave us,' I said the words slowly.

Cathy smiled, a wintry smile that never reached her eyes. 'You did that a year and four weeks ago, Heath. As you said, we both tried the world and I've moved on, I'm seeing someone now. I've got a date this Saturday for the school dance.'

She may as well have put a knife through my heart – no one could cut me like Cathy. The only person in the world that truly mattered to me and someone else is going to touch her.

'Who is he?' I asked in the most controlled voice I could muster.

She hesitated to tell me and then swallowed. 'Edgar Linton.'

'Edgar Linton,' I spat out. 'That privileged twat. Seriously?' I paced to the window, my hands fisting. *Get under control.* I turned back to see her hurrying to the staircase. She stopped on the bottom stair and turned back to me.

'Edgar's a gentleman and he wants to be with me. And I like him.'

'Really? You're going to do this?'

She turned and walked up the stairs away from me. My whole life was walking away from me.

Chapter 9 – The ecstasy and the agony

Heath

I thought I'd be sleeping at Wuthering Heights last night, but I slept in the spare room I'd been staying in for the past week since I came back into town to do the business deal. Aden – one of my friends from school – has his own place now and had been renting out the room to tourists as they travelled through the area. He was happy to have a break from playing host and cleaning, and happy to take my money instead. I made it worth his while. He worked in the local real estate office and as I came downstairs, he was heading off.

'Not working today?' he asked me, checking out my bed hair.

'Yeah, I'm like normal people though, I get into the office after 8am.'

He laughed. 'I've got an inspection with a couple who want to see the place before they go to work. Worth getting up for the commission if they buy it.' Aden was groomed to within an inch of his life. His dark hair was short back and sides, I could smell the cologne from the staircase and his pale grey suit, white business shirt and blue tie would have been a couple of months' salary.

'Speaking of wheeling and dealing, I was hoping I could rent for another week if that's cool?' I asked.

'Sure, stay as long as you like. Not interested in seeing a few properties to buy now that you've bought a business and are staying locally?' he suggested.

'Once a real estate agent always an agent,' I said with a sigh, and he grinned. 'I'm intending to own Wuthering Heights,' I boasted.

'Yeah? Hindley got anything to say about that?' Aden asked, his eyes wide with interest.

'I'll just let him know when the time is right,' I boasted, and then faked an evil laugh. Aden thought I was joking anyway, so may as well play along. 'But if I decide to buy, you'd be the only agent I come to.'

'Should bloody well think so,' he said, and grabbed his keys. 'Later.'

'Have a good day. Got your lunch and a clean hanky?' I joked, imitating a higher-pitched voice like his mother.

He gave me a rude finger sign and closed the front door behind him. I made a coffee and headed back upstairs for a shower. I was meeting Edgar today, just what I needed – a face to face with the guy who is with my girl. I hope I don't knock him out… it'll take a shitload of self-control. How long had they been going out?

I can't believe how it played out last night with Cathy. I keep going back through it thinking if I should have done it all differently, or what I should have done differently... damn, what a mess. I need to talk to her and get her to listen. I've planned out our whole future, that's what all this was for so we could get set up. So that I'd not only be the one she wants, but I'd be able to give her everything she wants.

God, I am such a dick. I had this great romantic fantasy playing out like I was going to come back into her life and prove myself to her, sweep her off her feet. Now I've lost her.

I stopped in my tracks. I realised what I had to do. If Cathy wants to play this game, then I'll fight fire with fire. She needs to look at me in a different light, through someone else's eyes. I hurried to dress and get to my new office; I had a call to make.

*****

Catherine

When Tilly picked me up this morning, Jace was in the car too – his regular ride must have turfed him. For me it was a blessing because Tilly wouldn't ask too much about Edgar in front of Jace – that was exclusive girls' talk – and I also wouldn't have to front up with the Heath story right away. She tried to read my face for signs and I gave her the thumbs up. Her eyes widened with excitement for me; bless her unselfish heart. God, I'm morphing into Nelly – I've got to get out morI sat in the back seat contributing now and then and tuning out in pure exhaustion. I had slept little last night. Just when I was in a happy place for the first time in over a year and could think about Edgar, him picking me up and me arriving at the dance on his arm, Heath – Mr see ya later – arrives and rains on my parade.

Last night I heard the door slam downstairs before I had even closed my bedroom door. I was devastated and angry, and I wanted him. I hoped he'd run up the stairs behind me to my room and hold me and tell me some story that made everything alright. I don't know what that story would be… where has he been for a whole year that he couldn't contact me and would let me suffer so? Maybe if he'd been in a coma, I'd be cool with that. Now he's gone again, and I've wounded him this time. He deserved it. I hate him. I love him, no, I hate him.

The sun came out and everything looked beautiful and green. I put down the window to inhale the air and got a chorus from the front seat to put it up.

'You'll mess up my hair,' Jace joked, and we gave him plenty. Thank God for Tilly and Jace.

It was in our third class for the day, Art with Ms Sumina, that Tilly and I got to talk. We could talk quietly while we painted – the assignment was a self-portrait in any style we liked. Tilly was a brilliant artist; she was doing her portrait in the Naturalism style. I had no talent for painting. I was doing a self-portrait like Picasso's *Weeping Woman*. Impressed? Yeah, thought so. So my face was all triangles and colour. I'd never looked better and it was pretty easy doing it that way.

'Wasn't he gorgeous yesterday?' Tilly sighed. 'They were both gorgeous. Your brother is so hot, and Edgar was just so smooth. So how did he get to the date question?'

'It took a while,' I told her. 'We danced around the family, the business, everything but the weather, although it was next on my list. Then he asked me out Saturday night, so I had to say 'no' because of the dance, so I asked him would he like to come and he said yes. I seriously can't believe he wants to go back to school.'

'And he'll pick you up in his car, and be wearing a suit? Be still my beating heart,' she sighed. Then she frowned at me and looked me up and down. 'I'm sensing you 're not as excited about this as you should be.'

Ms Sumina interrupted us as she made her way around the classroom checking on our self-portraits. She stood next to Tilly.

'Oh that's lovely, Matilda, just lovely. You have quite a talent, especially for light and shade.'

Tilly grinned. 'Thanks, Ms Sumina. I'm trying not to make myself look too good, it is naturalism after all.' We both laughed.

Then Ms Sumina moved next to me; I think my self-portrait scared her.

'Oh, well, that's a good effort, Catherine. Cubism is tricky.'

She was always so supportive. 'I'm more of an art theory rather than art practical girl, Ms Sumina,' I said, studying my painting.

'And there's nothing wrong with that,' she said, and gave me an encouraging nod and another glance at the painting. I suspect her self-portrait at this very moment would be '*The Scream*'. Never mind, as long as I passed the practical, I'd make up the grade with the theory.

'Spill it, Cathy,' Tilly said, reminding me what we're talking about.

I took a deep breath, lowered my voice, and began. 'You're right, I *was* so excited. Edgar is the complete package.'

'But?' Tilly asked impatiently.

'Heath arrived.'

'No!' she exclaimed, then dropped her voice again. 'No! Seriously? What the hell? Did he just show up?'

I nodded. 'Knocked on the front door after dinner and strode in like he was due back at that moment.'

'Where the hell has he been?'

'My question exactly!' I exclaimed. 'I don't know. He wanted to tell me, but I was so angry that I threw him out.'

'You did what?' Half of the class turned to look at us, and Ms Sumina gave us a warning look.

We sat quietly and painted like good art students for a few moments before starting up again.

'Technically, I didn't throw him out, he lives there too. I just told him I didn't care what he had to say since he took over a year to say it. I told him I was seeing Edgar.'

'You didn't?' she hissed.

'I did.'

'What did he do then?' Tilly asked, like she was watching a good soap opera unfold.

'He called Edgar a few names, and I turned and went upstairs and he stormed out.'

Tilly breathed out and returned to her painting. I could tell she was processing her advice for me. I dabbed at my painting and then glanced out the window. It was the bluest of blue days and the class in the year below us was out on the oval doing sport. I saw Isabella there with some of her friends. I wonder if Edgar told her when he got home that he was bringing me to the dance. I turned back to see Tilly looking at me.

'Okay, so are you going to go back to Heath?' she asked. 'Cancelling Saturday night with Edgar?'

'No way, Heath can get—' The bell rang over my words and we packed up.

I was aching for Heath. Damn him.

Chapter 10 – All is fair in love and business

Catherine

At our expectant look, Jace shook his head and lowered himself in the seat beside Tilly. I paused in between bites of my sandwich, expecting bad news. He tried to look nonchalant, like being rejected meant nothing, really.

'Oh no,' Tilly said, 'she said no?' We all subtly glanced at Isabella, who fortunately had her back to us from across the other side of the café.

Jace nodded. 'She's already hooked up with someone. Hardly surprising. It is the day before the dance,' he shrugged. 'Well, looks like it is you and me, babe,' he said to Tilly.

She grinned, thrilled, then masked it well with her come back.

'Even as besties we'll be more glamorous than most,' she said.

'Goes without saying,' Jace agreed, and they bumped fists.

'Except for me and Edgar,' I teased him. 'We are going to be too cool for school. I hope I don't trip over as we enter like I did at last year's dance – it was that stupid fitted dress, I couldn't move.'

Tilly laughed. 'It was kind of cute though, especially when Heath grabbed you and swept you off your feet rescuing you in that dramatic dip. Got a round of applause.' She realised what she had said and stopped smiling. 'But that's so last year.'

'So last year,' I agreed, echoing Tilly's words and remembering that romantic moment. Heath always had his fan club – the girls who thought him moody, dark and hot. The theme last year was strangely close to home – witches, warlocks and vampires. Heath and I went as vampires with Heath dashing in his suit and theatrical black cape, me in my way too fitted Morticia outfit.

'Yep, so last year,' I whispered again and then I noticed Tilly and Jace looking at me. 'To this year's theme.' I raised my water glass in a toast.

'To being glamorous,' Tilly said, much happier now than she was this morning now that she not only had a date for the dance, but it was Jace. She didn't miss the glance Jace gave over his shoulder towards Isabella. He still didn't see Tilly… just looked right through her.

*****

Edgar

I had a meeting in fifteen minutes with the directors and Heath Earnshaw – yeah, the guy who thinks Cathy is his – but I detoured through the mortuary; I liked to catch up with the different teams every day. I headed to the basement to catch up with our blood collecting team in the lab. The staff upstairs who work for the funeral business don't know about the blood business, they don't need to know. I like to mingle with the blood business staff – they were all sanguineous Immortalis, vampires like I would be one day. As I entered, I saw a middle-aged guy on the slab with tubes feeding him embalming fluid. He had already been drained of blood.

'A-type,' Tasman said before I could ask what came out of him.

'Nice drop. The lab guys are getting faster,' I said. 'We used to wait days for that info.'

'They're probably not busy enough,' he said with a wink and a laugh.

'Yeah, that'll get back,' I teased him. He had the vampire glow about him, preserved in his mid-twenties and beautiful forever. He hadn't planned to go through the Conversion until he hit thirty but his wife got cancer when she was twenty-five, so they both went through it early and now will never be separated. He loved his work, the company loved him, and his stunning wife worked front of house.

I checked out the vials of blood that we would send over to the Earnshaws shortly, so they could add the finishing touches, bottle, and label the 'blood wine' for customers. We don't get involved in that, except that we keep some for ourselves and the staff. The Earnshaws pay us for the blood, we supply it, they keep the client records and sell and deliver wine and blood if clients want it. It's a marriage made in heaven and under the radar.

There's money in it too, trust me. It's not dissimilar to the wine industry – good blood could be purchased for a good price and top-shelf blood was available for those wishing to pay for it or celebrations and special occasions.

This week the O'Connor family loss was our gain – thirty-five-year-old, Daniel O'Connor tragically killed in a motorcycle accident was a B-negative blood type. Delicious, rare and tantalising, it would fetch a good price. Sorry for your loss O'Connors but thanks. Less than two per cent of the population have B-negative and the odds of getting it if hunting yourself are extremely slim. For the handsome price of $250 a bottle upwards, you could have it on your own top-shelf.

Blood type O-positive was the most common with nearly 40 per cent of the population sporting this blood in their veins, so for everyday use customers would fork out between $6 to $10 a bottle, or less if they wanted to buy it in bulk which made it even more affordable. Trust me, we're always grateful for any blood but especially grateful for the top-shelf stuff.

The Moors has a sizeable population of sanguineous Immortalis successfully living with the Saps and contributing to society. So, if we keep supply up, there's no need for the carnage in the town. It is a win, win for everyone. Until Hindley took charge a few months ago.

'Done', Tasman said, removing the embalming tubes.

'Nice work,' I said. The corpse looked flushed and clean

'Well, leave you to it,' I said. 'Got a meeting.'

'Poor you,' Tasman said in sympathy.

I laughed and headed up the stairs. I could tell from the moment I entered the boardroom that Dad was not happy about something. Turned out to be about Hindley, no surprise there.

'What's he done now?' I asked, coming in on the end of a conversation. I could have guessed. Dad had no patience for Hindley, didn't want to even say his name, so our Mortuary Director, Karl Rivard, answered.

'Demanded a bigger cut,' he said, tapping his fingers on the boardroom table. He sat back in the chair and studied me. 'He believes we can't live without his company bottling and selling the wine, but they can live without us.' Karl's presence was imposing – he was a large, fit and dark man with an angular face and bright blue eyes. He was one of us; Dad trusted him implicitly.

'I'd like to see it,' I said. 'What's he going to do, run around and empty corpses himself?' I scoffed but I wouldn't have put it past him.

'There was an attack a few days ago… just saying,' Karl added.

'I wondered,' Dad said. 'Edgar tells me that Hindley converted.'

'No ceremony, but he's definitely gone over,' I said. I went to the window and stood at the opposite end to Dad, who was staring out over the car park.

'Makes me wonder if he has a potential new business partner,' Karl said.

Dad nodded. 'Crossed my mind, too. The only other mortuary run by members of our culture is in the next village – but approaching them would be risky unless they expressed interest first.'

'So what's Heath Earnshaw wanting to discuss with us today?' Dad cut to the chase with a glance at his watch. Heath was due at any minute.

'He has a business option he'd like to present us, apparently. He's bringing a couple of colleagues, not Immortalis.'

Dad stirred at the window. 'They've arrived,' he said as we watched a black car pull up.

'He's matured,' Dad said, 'he looks like—'

He hesitated. 'Money?' I suggested.

'Yes,' Dad agreed. Heath's suit was made to order, his shoes were quality and the two colleagues he was with were similarly suited. He was a lot different from the rough hooligan I remembered.

A few moments later the receptionist showed the three guys through to the boardroom. Heath led the way – tall, presentable and confident even if it was a bluff. He introduced the guy behind him as his business partner and I.T. General Manger, Conrad Suter – late twenties, thin in all things – body, glasses and hair; and lawyer Miles Gailbraith, an older guy.

Heath extended his hand to me and we shook. 'Edgar, Mr Linton, Karl, thank you for taking the time to see us,' he said. *Smooth.* After pleasantries, Heath cut to the chase.

'I've bought a private blood bank and I'd like to do talk with you about doing business together. I need a stock of blood, and we can store and distribute it.'

Timing was everything.

Chapter 11 - Saturday, at last.

Catherine

Shopping should be a school subject – Tilly would be an A-student. I would get a B – I'm good but she has endurance that I don't have, she's a shopping athlete. No seriously, this idea has legs – you learn how to budget, how to hunt for items, how to be discerning, how to live within your means, how to talk with people, and how to give up with good humour. At sunrise, okay, when the shops opened – it just felt like sunrise – in search of school dance dresses, we drove to nearby Bradford and worked those shopping malls and centres like there was no tomorrow. At this stage there wasn't given the dance was tonight. It was kind of exciting, we had a lot of fun and we both really got into it. For at least ten minutes every hour, I forgot about Heath while I shopped for a dress to wear with Edgar.

Where did he go last night? Was he with anyone? Why didn't he follow me upstairs and beg me to listen to him? I hate him. God, he looked so good. Just kill me now.

While fuelling up – ice coffee with caramel and whipped

cream for Tilly (skinny cow) and an All Berry Bang juice for me – we made a major decision; to rent a dress! Nelly would be so proud of me for not wasting money, and it's not that I didn't find good dresses, I just didn't find one that was going to make Edgar Linton stop in the doorway and gasp at how amazing I looked. So we went to *Glam Corner*, that's the name of the store, and we scored.

I found the most gorgeous long silver dress with an off-shoulder neckline; it was fitted to my hips and then it came out in a full skirt that swished… I love the swish. Tilly hired a rose gold floor-skimming gown with a scooped neckline, thin straps and a really amazing cowl back. We both had money left for shoes, so we bought those… you can't have enough shoes. It was going to be amazing, Edgar and Jace would like so handsome in their suits and we felt great about our dresses.

I wondered what it would be like to wear this dress with Heath.

*****

Later that afternoon, for the first time in days, I was home at the same times as Hindley. He arrived as Nelly and I were returning from a walk – it was a short walk. Nelly didn't go far these days. His strength and beauty drew Nelly in – he really did glow since the Conversion. His eyes were such a beautiful green, even his smile looked better. If only he was as nice as he looked.

'Going with anyone to the school dance?' he asked, and

sat down opposite as Nelly cut an apple cake she had made earlier.

I poured the tea and waited for his reaction. 'I'm going with Edgar.'

'Edgar! Edgar Linton?' he exclaimed.

'That's him,' I said.

'That's brilliant,' he said, surprising me.

'Why?' I asked, suspiciously.

'It will be good for business, well done,' he said, taking the offered cup of tea with a nod. I wasn't sure if his appetite extended to anything further than blood at this stage, but he wolfed down Nelly's apple cake like it was fresh from an artery.

'He's a lovely young man,' Nelly agreed. 'As is Heath.'

I saw Hindley's jaw lock.

'Heath came here,' I said. 'On Thursday night.'

'So he's crawled back into town, has he?' Hindley asked, a pleased smirk on his face.

'Trust me, there was no crawling involved. He's bought a business,' I said.

'He looked so different,' Nelly agreed, 'like he'd aged five years and was a responsible adult.'

'Why did you go through the Conversion without a celebration, and not in the moon phase? Must have been super painful,' I asked Hindley, changing the subject.

'It was, but I wanted to get it done and get to work. I'm changing things, Cathy, making them better for our family. I'm going to celebrate my Conversion in London later this month, you're both welcome,' he said, with a smile to Nelly.

‘Thank you, dear,’ she said, ‘but I’ll leave it to you and your young friends to uphold the tradition without an old woman hanging around. Perhaps we could have a family dinner one night to celebrate.’

‘Sure,’ Hindley agreed. It would never happen.

‘I would have come and stayed with you while you were going through it,’ I said.

‘Thanks, Sis,’ he smiled. ‘The pain was all over in a few hours. Makes you feel alive going through that transition.’

‘Well, you look fantastic. Does it feel amazing now?’ I asked.

He grinned. ‘You have no idea. But that’s why I wanted to get moving… I don’t want to waste any time. I’ve got ideas and changes, plans—’

‘What changes exactly are you making?’ I asked Hindley, trying to keep the suspicion and displeasure out of my voice.

‘A balance of power,’ he said. ‘For too long now our family business has been fifty-fifty in profits, but we do the balance of the work. We clean the blood, bottle it, label it, do the marketing and distribution. All the Lintons do is pump it and provide it raw, and they do well out of that.’

I refilled my tea and topped up Nelly’s and Hindley’s.

‘If you had spent more time with Dad learning the business you’d know that’s not true,’ I said, trying to not sound preachy. ‘We’d have no source of blood if it wasn’t for them. The Lintons get burials from all around this area including from Bradford. People who were born here or have family plots here or just want to be buried here. I think the figure last year was about 1500 burials for the year.’

'Good grief,' Nelly said, 'that's about 25 bodies a week.'

I nodded. 'Huge. And Dad said at a normal funeral parlour they wouldn't prepare bodies unless the family wanted an open casket. But because of the business, the Lintons drain every single body and refill it so they can supply us blood.' I sounded like Edgar had prepared me, but he hadn't. Dad had taught us about this – well, Heath and I since Hindley rarely took part in the business lessons.

'Yeah, I know about arterial embalming,' Hindley said, impatiently, 'and the work the make-up chic does.'

'Then you know the draining takes about an hour and putting the new fluid in takes about another hour, then the makeup artist prepares the face so it looks natural again. So all that costs them money and time – for fluid, for staff, wages, facilities, you know the story,' I said and shrugged.

'Yeah, well our role is just as laborious, trust me I've done the math,' he said, not wanting to hear me.

Nelly rose and excused herself to do some chores. I think she was happy to get away from our discussion.

'Just a thought,' I said, 'if the Lintons get cheesed off with us and leave, we've got no blood, just the wine business. They can find another distributor or do it themselves… they don't really need us as much as we need them.'

'I think you'll find they need us more than you know. Our bottler, our distribution networks, our distributors, marketers, the mailing list – that's decades of work and can't be replicated overnight. Trust me, Cathy, I'm growing this business and they can come for the ride or not.' He smiled. 'But they'll come.'

‘And if they don’t? Do our clients just go direct to them or—’

‘Some will,’ Hindley cut me off. ‘But it will be worse than that. If there’s no blood bottled and distributed, then for the first time in a long time some of the good citizens of The Moors will die or start to hunt.’

Chapter 12 – The dance

Catherine

I couldn't breathe. I think I had worked myself up too much about the date with Edgar and about Heath being back, about our people becoming bloodsuckers again due to lack of supply… I just want to stop my brain from churning for five minutes and chill out. To make it worse, it was quiet, deathly quiet. I never liked it when the wind didn't howl – it wasn't normal on the moors.

I had a shower, shaved and plucked every conceivable hair that was unwelcome, and began on my makeup. The natural look that every guy said he loved took so long – oh, the irony. But honestly, I wore little anyway. I blow-dried my hair, put on my jewellery, and then slipped on the dress. Yes! It looked hot even if I say so myself. I am so ready.

I was super excited, but I missed Heath. On second thoughts, maybe I'll never be ready to see someone else.

*****

Edgar

I never thought I'd get out of the house. Mum was wrapped that I had a date with Cathy, Dad was worried about the Heath connection, and yeah, it had crossed my mind a few hundred times since I saw Heath at the office. But tonight, I don't give a shit. I'm going to be with Cathy. Beautiful Cathy. I can't believe our family estates have been next to each other forever, and our family businesses have been entwined since the last century and yet, Cathy and I aren't already together. It's destiny.

If Heath hadn't come on the scene all those years ago she would have seen me and been with me a lot earlier and Charlotte would never have been on my radar. Tonight, I'll have her in my car and my arms. I had the car cleaned today, suit dry cleaned, hair cut… Cathy was worth the effort. I can't believe how nervous I am… insane. I've known Cathy since we were kids. I remember her from the grade below me at school and seeing her when I would go with my dad to her parent's business. It was pretty much once we got to high school that we never said much to each other, not until the fundraising campaign we had to do together. Why was that? Heath.

I started the car and headed out of our place and across the moors to Cathy's home, Wuthering Heights. Our houses were exactly six and a half kilometres apart and yet with nothing in between but the moors, it felt like we lived in different towns. Within a few minutes, her long drive came into view. Her home is higher than our house, perched on top of the hill. No wonder it gets beaten by the wind. It's not a super inviting place… especially since her parents died and it looks like three-quarters of the house is in darkness, with just some lights on along one side of the building. It's huge and dark looking, kind of brooding in a way. I pressed the buzzer at the gate and it opened; I drove through.

I felt like I was coming to get Cathy and take her to her rightful home, like everything until now had been practice. Nelly would be here too; I'd love Nelly to work back at our place. I want to skip this part and go straight to life ever after with Cathy. Too soon? Yeah, probably. Don't scare her off, just be cool, confident, calm… everything I was with Charlotte because I didn't care that much. Everything I'm not with Cathy.

I pulled up outside the front door and exited the car. Deep breath. I rang the doorbell.

******

Catherine

'Cathy,' Nelly called a moment after the doorbell rang. Thank God we haven't gone through the Conversion or he'd be able to hear my heartbeat from the front door!

'Coming,' I called back.

One more turn in the mirror – yep, as good as it's ever going to be. I stopped, no think positive, be positive.

'You look great, go get them, girl,' I told myself, and smiled at my reflection. Throughout high school it has always been Cathy and Heath, Heath and Cathy, but that time was over. This is a new start, it's Cathy and Edgar now and it is going to be a great night. I took a deep breath to settle the butterflies and left the room. It's time.

I couldn't see him for a few moments, Nelly had Edgar swallowed in an embrace. He stepped back laughing and he looked beautiful, like he was straight from a catwalk. He wore a fitted dark suit with a white bow tie and a crisp white shirt. You could see a reflection in his beautiful shiny black shoes and he looked so handsome, and then he looked up at me and he stopped still.

Nelly looked up as well and clasped her hands together as I came down the stairs.

'Cathy, you look beautiful,' she said. 'You both do,' and she reached for her handkerchief buried somewhere in her chest pocket and dabbed her eyes. Dear Nelly.

'Hello,' Edgar said.

'Hello,' I said back to him and grinned. I arrived beside him, and he leant in to kiss me on the cheek.

'You look stunning,' he said, and then held up his hand for me to wait. He dashed back out, and I heard his car door opening and closing. Edgar returned with an enormous bunch of white roses tied with a cream silk ribbon.

'Oh my,' Nelly said.

'They are stunning, thank you,' I said, taking them and inhaling their scent. One dozen long-stemmed white roses. Perfect.

'Now let me put those in water and you two head off,' Nelly said, accepting the flowers from me. 'Got your key, Cathy?'

I nodded. 'Night, Nelly.'

'Goodnight darling, enjoy yourself now,' she said and kissed me on the cheek. She turned to Edgar. 'I hope we see a lot more of you, young man.'

'Me too, Nelly,' he said and crooked his arm. I slipped my hand through, and he escorted me to the car as Nelly closed the door behind us. He opened the front door to his luxury car and I lowered myself in as gracefully as I could with the slinky dress on. While he went around the car to the driver's door, I took a deep breath since I forgot to breathe for the last five minutes. He slipped in beside me and we were together in his car, in the small surrounds with so much energy in the air between us; I think the oxygen was depleting. I felt light-headed. I didn't mean to look at his lips but I did, and then I had to sit back and look straight ahead and focus on the dashboard. I wondered how I was going to survive the night.

'Well, I know the way,' he said, starting the car, and we laughed.

And then we drove off, Edgar in charge of the car and my heart.

*****

You couldn't miss our school hall, it was lit with Hollywood beams crossing in front of it. Glamorous indeed. Fairy lights filled the nearby trees.

'Wow, the social committee's gone all out,' I said, admiring their work.

'Looks great,' Edgar agreed, and laughed. 'Check that out.'

The committee had organised false paparazzi who were running around in packs, taking photos with huge cameras and flashes going off.

'Very cool,' I agreed.

We pulled into a car park along the road and sat for just a moment watching the glamourous couples heading to the hall.

'Ready?' Edgar asked.

'I am.'

He exited and before I had reached for the door handle, he was opening my door and offering me his hand to step out of the car. I saw the 'paparazzi' running over to us and even though it was super corny, it was fun. Edgar locked the car and taking my hand close to his chest, we walked in.

I could see some of my classmates already staring at us. It had only been six months since Edgar and Charlotte had graduated and here he was on my arm; everyone remembered him, of course. And they remembered Heath. I could almost hear the buzz of rumours circulating. If I had my Immortalis' senses, I'd hear what they were saying.

We walked along the footpath and Edgar smiled at me.

'Did I mention you look beautiful?'

'I'm sure if you did I can't remember. No harm saying it again,' I said, teasing him and he laughed.

'You look absolutely beautiful,' he said. 'I'm glad you asked me to escort you.'

'Me too,' I said, 'and you look dashing!' I gave him a smile that hopefully said it all. It was all I could come up with and stay upright and breathing. Then I spotted Tilly and Jace.

They looked fantastic together and if Jace didn't see Tilly tonight when she looked so beautiful, then he would never see her, ever.

'Oh my God, you two look great,' Tilly gushed and accepted a kiss on the cheek from Edgar. The boys shook hands.

'You two look fantastic too, a hot couple,' I said. 'How good is this hall?'

Inside was all gold, white and silver decorations with huge mirror balls, and flashing up on the walls were glamorous images of Hollywood stars.

'Better be careful you two,' Jace said, looking at my silver dress and Tilly's gold rose dress. 'With this colour scheme, we won't be able to find you in the hall. Let's dance, Tilly.' And he whirled her away, leaving us standing inside the doorway.

Edgar led me over to get a drink and some of my friends came over to say hello and greet Edgar. Everyone looked so fantastic that I couldn't concentrate on the conversation while watching.

Then a slow number came on and the DJ invited us to give this dance to someone special. Edgar put his glass down and turned to me.

'May I have this dance?' he asked. So old world charming.

'It would be my pleasure,' I said, and relinquished my glass to him. We walked to the dance floor and I couldn't believe that I was going to be dancing with Edgar Linton, the guy every girl in his grade last year wanted, and in the grades below, too. Not that Heath didn't have his admirers, but he could be moody and dark, whereas Edgar was aloof but charming. Big difference.

I placed my hand on his shoulder and the other in his hand and pulling me closer, he slowly led me around the floor as the lights gently blinked and bounced off the mirror balls and my dress reflected the glow. I could see Tilly and Jace dancing, thank goodness.

And then there was a buzz of voices again, and some activity near the entrance door. I couldn't see because of couples dancing in front of me and I didn't really care. Until the crowd parted enough and I could see the couple that just entered.

My heart snapped in two. Isabella just entered with her date. Heath.

*****

Heath

She is the first and only thing I saw as I entered the room. My love, there dancing and touching Edgar Linton. If my eyes could have burnt him to the ground and melted her with my gaze, God knows I would have. I didn't notice the surrounding din, and then Isabella was saying my name and I looked at her.

'Shall we dance or would you like a drink?' she asked.

I should ask that question. Step up, I told myself. I needed Isabella on my side for this business deal. Didn't want her running home to her daddy and Edgar all upset.

'Sorry, Bella,' I said. 'Will you allow me the pleasure of this dance?' I offered a little bow and she giggled. God, she was so sweet I could kill her here and now. Save that blood for down the track. Bet she's one of those rare types as well – an AB-negative, maybe. Although I heard that type can be spicy. Forget it, stay on track.

I took her hand, and we joined the dance floor.

'Everyone is looking at you because you look so beautiful,' I whispered to her and she blushed. Whatever it takes.

'Thank you,' she said demurely. 'I think they are looking because we're a couple no one expected to see! And you do look strikingly handsome.'

I pulled her closer, mainly to shut her up. And then we neared Edgar and Cathy. We were so close.

Edgar greeted me with a smile and a nod. I couldn't read how he felt about me being with his sister. I'd happily swap partners. Catherine, my Cathy.

Cathy looked wounded. Her look, her initial reaction, sent a jolt of pain to my heart. Why were we doing this to each other? I came back to you. Yes, I was an idiot… I should have made contact, but I had a plan. I knew what that was; she didn't. I swallowed and nodded at her and she looked away.

Mission accomplished. Two can play at breaking hearts, beautiful girl. Every set of eyes in the room was watching us, watching her for a reaction and I've got to hand it to her, she was grace under fire; she would not put on a show. Cathy turned away, refocussing on Edgar, giving him a smile she should have been giving me. Running her little hand along his shoulder, she clasped his other hand, I could see her knuckles were white. She said something to him and they shared a smile.

At that moment, I fucking hated her. *What are you doing?*

I returned my focus to Isabella. She was beautiful but so what? There were a lot of beautiful people in the world, she wasn't Catherine. I tried to concentrate on her, to make her night special. But every chance I could get, I couldn't help but glimpse in Cathy's direction.

Come back to me, Cathy. Edgar could not in his entire lifetime love you as much as I love you in one day.

*****

Catherine

Agony. I could not wait for the night to be over so I could lie in my bed and cry my heart out. When Heath came through that door with Isabella on his arm, he plunged a knife into my heart. I felt it; I thought I was going to fall over. It was only because Edgar was holding me upright that I didn't. I tried not to look at the two of them together, but I'm drawn back to them like a horror movie that you can't bear to watch but you can't look away.

Heath knows how to get to me every time. Our sufferings are so entangled that sometimes I can't free myself from his pain, but tonight, this agony is all mine. Edgar was so gorgeous and attentive, and so lovely, but my head was full of Heath and this treachery. He knew what bringing

Isabella to the dance would do to me. What have I done to deserve this?

I turn away from Heath; I just can't look at him anymore without breaking down and I can't do that to Edgar, I won't do that to him. I was operating on remote control like I was outside my body and just getting through the night – smiling, dancing, laughing at my friend's jokes. Poor Edgar, I hope he is having a good time and thinks I am reasonable company. I just want to go home.

After an hour or so the shock had diminished, my anger has increased and I've cast off Heath's attempt to wound me for what it was – pathetic. You have Isabella, Heath. If she will have you, then be happy with her. I release you.

Chapter 13 – Raw pain

Catherine

I watched Edgar drive off looking like a high-fashion model in an expensive car, and then I went in, locked the door and kept the noise down so I wouldn't wake Nelly even though her room was in a different wing. I glanced down the hallway to what once was Heath's room. The door was open and the lights were off – he hadn't returned here and I wasn't expecting him to come back. Hindley's door was the same – open with the lights out. I wonder where he's staying tonight or maybe because he's had his Conversion he doesn't sleep at all now, well not conventionally. He's probably sleeping in the cool cellar at work, having knocked over enough grape wine and blood wine for a small nation.

I went through to the kitchen and helped myself to half a glass of juice. On the table were Edgar's beautiful roses in a crystal vase. I inhaled their scent. Why did Heath have to come back now? His timing was shit. I drained the juice, rinsed the glass, and headed upstairs. My room was in darkness so I flicked on my bedside lamp and headed to the bathroom to take a quick shower; I needed to wash off my makeup and all the night's tension. What a night – holy crap, I thought as I relaxed under the hot stream of water. Tilly and I had plenty to talk about the next morning. I reluctantly pulled myself out of the shower and, drying off, headed back to my room. It was weird to have the house so empty; it was once a full house – Mum, Dad, Nelly, me, Hindley, Heath, our gardener, cleaner – now it was just Nelly and me. Quiet as a tomb.

I threw on my singlet and boxer shorts and went to close the bedroom curtains. It's not like anyone could see in – there was no one around for miles and miles and no houses nearby, but I didn't want the morning sun waking me early if I got to sleep. The moon was lovely tonight. Not a Conversion moon, but I had a Conversion party next week that would be fun. At least one of my brother's friends invited me to his Conversion since Hindley hasn't had his party yet! They were all four years older than me, but I've known them since Hindley started school.

I looked towards the enormous tree outside my window that gave me grief every time a storm struck, but it was still tonight; the wind was taking the night off. I turned to go and a shape, a man, stepped out from behind the tree. I gasped. My heart was thundering. I slid beside the curtain to peek down.

It was Heath. What the…? He had some nerve showing up and some nerve scaring the shit out of me. I pulled the curtains closed and turned off the bedside lamp.

I climbed into bed and tried to forget he was there.

Impossible. A few minutes later, I heard small stones hitting the window. He has a frigging key!

'Just let yourself in Heath!' I said, to the room, no one heard me. Again, another small tap against the window.

'I'm not coming,' I muttered. 'Go away.'

I waited. There was no sound, but that made me more nervous. I was just about to head to the window to peak out when I heard my window casement going up. I sat bolt upright in bed and Heath swung through the window.

'What the hell are you doing? You've got a key, you don't need to play Spiderman,' I snapped at him as I got up and headed towards my bedroom door. 'Now get out of my room,' I said, unlocking the door and opening it for him.

'You've bolted the front door,' he said matter-of-factly. 'But I'm not here to sleep, I've got a place to stay.'

I knew he was staying somewhere else, but I thought it was temporary. Had he officially left Wuthering Heights?

He walked towards me, grabbed the edge of the bedroom door and closed it. He stood close enough to grab me, but he didn't dare.

'I came to see you, Cathy. We need to talk and you need to hear me out.'

I folded my arms and held my ground. 'See, that's where you're wrong,' I said, using all the courage I could muster, the courage to not throw myself at him, that is.

He crossed his arms across his chest, imitating me and looking defiant and gorgeous. Damn him.

I was so relieved to see him I felt myself choking up, but there was no way I'd admit that. I cleared my throat to speak. 'You left me, so that's you calling it off. You left for over a year and I've moved on.'

He scowled at me, but didn't interrupt.

'And tonight you saw the man I've moved on with. So, Heath, I don't have to hear you out because nothing you say will interest me.' I turned and returned to the window, pushing it closed. 'So why don't you go via the front door and head up the road further and throw stones at Isabella's bedroom window since she's your new girlfriend.'

I got a bit worked up as I spoke and spat the words out like they were poison. I was so angry, I didn't know how long it would take me to get over his desertion let alone bringing Isabella to the dance, but it sure as hell wasn't a couple of days.

He moved towards me at the window and I sidestepped him. I heard him sigh with frustration.

'You and I both know I'm not even remotely interested in Isabella and there's a reason I went away. You fuelled it. So, I'm not leaving, Cathy, until—'

'Fine, then I'll leave.' I churlishly returned to my bed, grabbed my pillow, and turned for the door exiting before he could reach me. I heard him hiss my name as his fingers brushed my arm before I raced out of the room. He followed me down the hallway and I went into Mum and Dad's room, turning on the light and quickly locking the door behind me. He hit the door and tried the lock.

'Damn you, Cathy, open the door,' he said in a hushed but urgent voice.

'Go away Heath, you'll wake Nelly. Go and continue

your new life, the life without me,' I said and turned off the light, removing the sliver of light beneath the doorway and leaving him in a completely dark hallway. He tried the lock again, and I heard him swear. I waited, pressed up against the door and so did he. A few moments later I heard his footsteps retreating down the stairs. I didn't come out of Mum and Dad's room; it felt strangely peaceful in there and I could use their comfort at the moment. I lay on Mum's side of the bed and buried my face in the pillow.

I heard nothing more.

Chapter 14 – Friends and enemies

Catherine

The week went by fast. Normally that doesn't happen when your heart sick, in pain and your whole life is upside down, but I kept frantically busy so that the aching couldn't catch up with me. I was seeing Edgar again this weekend. I rang him on Sunday to thank him for coming with me and we talked for ages. He's just so great, if only Heath wasn't in my head and heart, ah, shut up me. Heath appeared again on Monday night outside my window. I closed the curtains on him and he left. If he is waiting for me to let him in, then he'll be standing outside there forever, and I keep my bedroom door locked. I can't believe he is back and still alive. I want to kill him for all the times I worried he was dead over the past year. I'm talking about Heath again, I'm pathetic.

At least he took the hint and didn't show up for the rest of the week. Tuesday, Wednesday and Thursday I looked out for him outside my room but he hasn't been there. I can't believe it – if he was serious about telling me his story and winning me back he should be outside pining away, looking miserable. I wonder if he got scared off – I am sure I saw a wild dog roaming around our grounds in the dark… the flash of yellow eyes and a low growl was enough to send chills up my spine and saw me scurrying back inside when I contemplated a late-night walk. They used to live wild on the moors. Some people said they were demons, souls that couldn't rest. Others said they were protectors. Dad said that was just a myth or folklore about the dog being connected to witches and black magic. Dad believed they were there, living wild – he saw a pack one day when walking. They didn't come near him, luckily, since Dad didn't have any special powers to defend himself as a Sap.

Forget Heath, it was Friday and tonight Tilly and I were going to a Conversion party, so exciting. Well, Tilly thinks it is a 21st party of course; it will be good for her to take her mind off Jace since he has shown no interest in her since the dance – men! Whatever, it will be great fun; these parties always are. This was a Youth Dew party – Hindley's friend, Daniel Evermore, was taking the plunge. It kind of worried me with Hindley's friends that they were too impetuous to think through their decisions. They just wanted power and beauty and they wanted it now. I know Daniel's parents probably went through all that with him, but I hope Hindley's Conversion didn't rush Dan into it.

It was a penumbral moon so there were probably Conversions going on all over the country. Dan would be finished the process now and preparing for the party tonight. It's an extensive process – he had to fast from Wednesday morning and go into The Dome that night at midnight. He stayed in complete darkness all day Thursday, super freaky, to allow his body to rid itself of all residue light. Then at nightfall Thursday, when the eclipse began, his official Conversion started as the moon passed through the earth's shadow between 8pm and 1am, creating a penumbral lunar eclipse. I sound so scientific! But it's a good way to do it because there's lots of time to convert and the slowness helps minimise pain.

During this time the elder gave him the bite and then he tasted the blood of the elder. His body pump that blood through his system for the next four hours of the eclipse and he'd feel heightened pain, joy, vision, sound, all that, so I've been told. Then when the eclipse finished, about 1am Friday – this morning – his Conversion was complete. He would have gone out with the elder or a few of them and experienced the remaining night and early morning with his new senses. Tonight we'll do the official celebrating at his '21st party'.

We have the Conversion ceremonies at The Dome – several families have their own rooms which for normal people just look like a planetarium would, a great place to watch the moon and the stars. But we reserved them for Conversions when needed. But The Dome is the place that most people in the village use because it's been the chosen site for centuries and it's on a secure estate of one of the oldest vampire families in The Moors. The elder of the family does the official ceremony. You can have family members with you or do it alone. Most people do it alone and then emerge converted like a caterpillar from a chrysalis into a butterfly. How poetic, yeah!

It hasn't always gone well. Sometimes the Conversion is too much for the person going through it and they go a little crazy in the dark or when the first blood hits them. That's why it's good that an elder stages them because they are super strong and can manage the 'newborn'. I couldn't wait to see Dan; just after The Conversion, the person always has the most beautiful glow, their eyes are so bright – it's the best part. The other great part is that tonight Tilly and I can just dance and have fun. Heath and Edgar are not part of this group and won't be there. I can have the night off from stressing out.

*****

Heath

Well, well, well. At the end of my first week in my new office, in my new job, guess who shows up at reception? Hindley Earnshaw, my big 'brother'. Thank God we don't share the same blood, that would be a burden to live with. My receptionist, Sophie, calls me to announce him. I wonder if he heard about my meeting with the Lintons or that I'd sent them a formal partnership offer.

I have a large block of TV monitors in my office showing all the different angles of the business and I watch him charming her as he waits for me. She smiles, flicks her hair, looks demure, all the usual crap. I'm pretty sure he's converted – even in the black and white monitors he looks different if you know what you are looking for; I'll know as soon as I see him.

I take a large breath, straighten my tie and go out to meet Hindley. As I enter the room, he moves away from the reception desk and sizes me up.

'Lost?' I ask.

He laughs. 'My sources told me you were back.'

'Well, they're worth their weight in salary, aren't they, bro?' I said. He had definitely undergone the Conversion; he was glowing with life.

'Are you going to ask me in?' he asked with a nod down the hallway to where I just came from.

'No.'

He glanced at Sophie, trying to read if she was one of 'us' or a Sap.

'Sophie, will you just let Miles and Conrad know the Lintons received the contract and the appointment is confirmed, please?' I ask her.

'Sure, Mr Earnshaw,' she said, rising and heading down the hall. I turned back to Heath. 'You had thirteen years to welcome me into your father's home and I don't remember one kind word you said to me in that entire time. So I'm sure as shit not welcoming you here.'

'Oh, boo hoo,' he said.

'What do you want, Hindley? Catch up on old times? Relive all our happy memories?'

I thought back to the number of times Hindley had thrashed me or blamed me for things he did. Sure all siblings did that, but this was different. From the moment I entered Wuthering Heights with Dad, Hindley hated me. Every chance he got, he would take it out on me and he was a big kid; I didn't catch up in height and weight until I was in my mid-teens. It didn't help that Dad loved me – a stranger – as much as his first-born son. Thank God for Cathy or I would have run away years ago and tried my luck back on the streets. She made Wuthering Heights a home, my home. Wherever she is, is my home. As for Hindley, I'll have his blood one day, and I don't care how long I wait. At least with him having undergone the Conversion, he won't die before I get to destroy him myself.

Watching Sophie leave, I turned back to Hindley. 'So you've had the Conversion. You look better for it.' I threw him a bone. He didn't know how to take a compliment from me, it put him on the back foot. That was the plan.

He shrugged. Then I noticed the scratches on his hands.

'You've hunted!' As I suspected. 'Why, when you've got top-shelf blood? That's just hard work and too dirty for you, surely,' I mocked him.

He looked at his hands and started to deny it, then I suspect because he didn't give a shit what I thought, he just blurted it out.

'I wanted to try it – basic instinct.'

'And?' I asked.

It's a rush, but who can be arsed cleaning up and getting rid of the body.'

Cleaning up. Body. He didn't have an animal? Then it dawned on me.

I lowered my voice. 'Shit, you killed that guy they found at the cemetery, the druggie.'

Hindley smirked and crossed his arms over his chest.

'I did the community a favour. He's been selling that shit to kids around here for years, he's a grub. Tasted like it too.' He grimaced. 'They'll forget it soon enough, they're already blaming it on his druggie mates.'

I shook my head. 'Clever… the extra blood, was it wine blood so they didn't find him drained?'

Hindley grinned. 'I grabbed some O-type. Ripped open his throat so it made sense why he'd lost a lot of blood after I drank my share, and then just soaked the area in wine blood. Won't happen again,' Hindley said. 'Going for top-shelf from now on, as you said.'

'It'll work unless the autopsy shows two different blood types,' I reminded him.

He scoffed. 'I don't think they'll be looking too closely at the spilt blood of a druggie.'

It was the longest conversation we'd ever had in our lives and we spoke like friends, and then that seemed to dawn on us both as we went back into our natural roles.

He uncrossed his arms and leant against the counter, sizing me up. 'You're trying to crack into my business.'

'No, I'm not trying to expand our *family* business,' I said, knowing that would work him up. Let's see how much control he's got with his new powers. I smile at him and say: 'I'm trying to put you out of business.'

He snarled, like some wild dog. His lip curled up at one end.

'You'd destroy my father's business, the hand that fed you?' he asked, his eyes narrowed with hate.

I put my hands in my suit pocket and rocked on my heels,

keeping my cool because I knew that would piss him off too – it took little to piss Hindley off, he was wound tight.

'Just the opposite,' I said. 'I plan to drive you out of business and save the Earnshaw and Linton business relationship put in place by our father and our forefathers. Dad would be proud.'

He pointed his finger at me and leaned forward. 'Let's get one thing straight, my father is not your father. You're just some gutter trash he picked up, dusted off and leant a bedroom too. The loan is over.'

'That so?' I asked. 'And yet he taught me the business, and in his will named the three of us as company executives when we come of age. You just got there first.'

'Yeah, and I'll look after the business until Cathy comes of age. I'm talking to my lawyer right now about how to get you out of the company.'

I shrugged. 'From what I hear, there'll be no business to hand over to Cathy at the rate you're going. Oh wait, there might be a few grapes left on the vine.'

That was it, I knew it would be. He charged at me with all his new vampire strength. His eyes flared bright, his teeth extended and he threw me against the wall with such power that a huge crack appeared in the plaster; it would have knocked out any ordinary man, perhaps that's what he was counting on.

He looked surprised that it hadn't impacted me. I smiled at him as he held me by the throat pressed against the wall. He saw my eyes, just a flash of what was behind them, it wiped the grin off his face.

For a moment, a look of fear and confusion crossed over his face. He released me and stepped back.

'What the fuck are you?' he said.

I had told Cathy that I found my heritage, but I didn't have the chance to tell her what it was. But now I knew why her dad had brought me home. One of his kind paired with my mother, a shapeshifter, and they were killed for it. He saved the hybrid kid; I know why too. Guilt.

I stood to full height, straightened out my neck and shoulders, and allowed myself to give him just one small preview of who I was. I gave him a full blast of my yellow eyes.

He stepped further back and looked at me with pure hatred.

'Werewolf!' he hissed.

'Oh, I'm better than that,' I said. 'Hybrid. Some might say the best of your clan and the best of mine.'

We both knew what that meant; I didn't have to undergo the Conversion, I already had the blood of both in my system and the moment I used them would be the moment they were here to stay, forever. I was testing my shapeshifter powers already; I hadn't warmed up to trying the blood-sucking side yet. I wanted to wait until Cathy had her Conversion so we could change at the same time, but that might not be possible if I had to defend myself.

Hindley's bravado returned and he flashed a smile at me. 'I knew you were gutter trash – a fucking hybrid. Never will your filthy clan take over my father's life work. Over my dead body,' he said, spitting the words out at me.

'I'm planning on that,' I said. 'Besides, your father knew

what I was. He rescued me out of guilt, do you want to know why?' I asked, straightening my tie again since he roughed me up.

He was busting to know but Sophie re-joined us and we both reined it in.

'This is not over,' he said in a low, threatening tone. He turned and left, slamming the door behind him.

If I had a bottle of blood wine for every time Hindley had said that to me, I'd have the best cellar in The Moors.

I turned to the now seated receptionist whose eyes were huge with concern.

'Sorry about that, Sophie,' I said. 'Best not to buzz him in next time. Just let security or me know and we'll go out and meet him.'

'Sure, Mr Earnshaw,' she said, biting her lower lip.

I loved getting under his skin; I'd be planning that for years. Now, I just had to tell Cathy what I was and what we could be together, what power we would have.

*****

Edgar

I want to ask Catherine to my house on Saturday night if that doesn't seem too forward. She hasn't been to Thrushcross Grange since she was a kid and dropped in with her father. I showed her the stables then, she loves to ride from what I remember. When Mum and Dad move away – and they will in the coming years – this will be my home, our home. Isabella will marry and leave, but I'm first born and Thrushcross Grange will be mine. I can see Cathy here, the house suits her. It's a grand old estate surrounded by groomed parkland and the rooms are light and well-lit. She can decorate as she sees fit when she is the lady of the house.

I stopped daydreaming as Dad tapped on my open office door, and I invited him in. He entered, closed the door and sat down in the chair opposite. He was good like that; even though he was the boss, he didn't just storm in or interrupt what you are doing.

'Heath's business proposal is good, very good,' he said. 'What do you think?'

I leant forward, folding my arms on the desk.

'Yeah, I hate to admit it but it's really good and makes sense for us.'

Dad laughed. 'Not a fan of Heath?'

I shrugged. 'I don't really know him. But we're both keen on Cathy.'

'Ah,' Dad said and sat back, crossing his legs. 'Mm, well, that could be a problem. I've been stalling Hindley's lawyer who keeps pushing for a response to Hindley's new proposal—'

'New price rise structure with us losing out, you mean?' I cut Dad off.

'That's it. I just hate to jump ship with the Earnshaws after all that history and century of goodwill. I wouldn't mind one more attempt to bring young Hindley around.'

'And if he doesn't come around?' I asked.

'I don't see how we can, or why we should continue to

do business with him. Heath's offered relationship is for as long as we want to make it, there's a much more logical fit for us to be involved with a blood bank than a winery… it's never going to raise suspicion if we're donating blood for the greater good, and technically he's still an Earnshaw.'

I nodded. 'Then let's stall them both and have one more negotiation attempt with Hindley.

Dad rose. 'I'll go set up another meeting with him. When are you taking Cathy out again?'

'Saturday,' I said, and smiled, even though I was trying to look cool about it. 'Thought I might ask her over for the day since you and Mum are away for the weekend.'

'Tell her it will all be hers one day,' he teased. 'Who could resist you and Thrushcross Grange?'

'Ha, thanks, I wish I was as confident,' I confessed. He gave me a smile and a nod, as though he remembered those days of insecurity and youth. With that, Dad left and I could see the future like it was written on the wall in front of me. Heath will run Hindley into the ground and Cathy will have to choose between Heath and Wuthering Heights, or me and Thrushcross Grange.

I had to win.

Chapter 15 – The party

Catherine

'This is the best party… since the last one,' Tilly said and giggled. She was the only person I know who could get high on fruit punch and sparkling water. I think it was just anything with bubbles really.

We topped up our drinks and took some time off the dance floor to check everything out. The hall Dan had hired for his Conversion and 21st party was packed, there must have been 200 people celebrating at his party. The DJ was brilliant and—

'Dan is gorgeous,' Tilly gushed, watching him dance.

'You think everyone is gorgeous,' I reminded her and we laughed. There were a lot of gorgeous guys here tonight – who would have thought Hindley's dorky friends would have grown up and turned out reasonably good! It'd be great if Tilly fell for one of Dan's friends who wasn't from our culture, you know, someone who was a Sap like Tilly. I looked out for one.

'Hey Sean's a really nice guy, you should meet him, I'll

introduce you,' I said, shouting near her ear and pointing out one of Hindley's friends who was a decent Sap. Tilly narrowed her eyes as she checked him out. Sean saw us looking and came over.

'Hi Cathy, long time no see, you look great,' he said, 'all grown up.'

I laughed. 'Funny guy,' I told him, he'd only seen me last month. He looked pretty hot though in a dark suit with an open white shirt and no tie. He'd gone all out for the Conversion Party.

'This is my best friend, Tilly.' I introduced them. They shook hands and sized each other up. They'd look great together, both fair and pretty – Sean would hate that description.

'Want to dance,' he asked both of us.

I shook my head. 'I need time out, but Tilly could dance forever.' And my work is done here. She smiled at me as he took her hand and led her out into the middle of the crowd working the dance floor and with a grin in her direction, I headed outside for some fresh air and quiet.

It was blissful and cool outside, the first time I had a chance to think which wasn't necessarily a good thing. I sat on the sandstone stairs of the old hall and breathed in the night. Behind me, the music thumped, but outside the sky was clear, the stars were bright and the wind was only a light hum in my ears. There was also a bit of extracurricular activity going on around both sides of the hall, but at least I couldn't see it.

And then Hindley appeared.

'Hey, taking time out too?' he asked. He breathed in deeply. 'Much cooler out here.'

I nodded. 'Good party, Dan looks great, glowing.'

'Yeah, he came through it easily,' he said and sat down on the stone step near me.

'I wish you'd taken the easy road. I hate to think of you in pain for hours,' I said.

He shrugged and smiled at me. 'It was worth it.'

'What's it like?' I asked, lowering my voice in case there were Saps around.

He thought about it for a moment. 'The procedure is freaky; the day spent in the dark is hard and you've got hours in your head. The elders don't like you playing music or anything because they want you to reflect,' he said, and scoffed. 'Later, you're lying there really weak because you haven't eaten, and then you get the blood and it's like your senses are on overload, as if you've never really been alive.'

I shivered. 'That's freaky but kind of exciting too.'

'I slept, so that was cool. The best thing to do is stay awake as long as you can before you go in and try to sleep through it. But when you wake up, you just have to lie there in the dark and wait until dusk. Then, two elders come in and talk you through your decision again. They can refuse to do it if they think you're not ready,' Hindley said.

'Well, that's kind of a good thing,' I suggested. 'Are they dressed like ceremonially?'

'Yeah, white robes, horns on their heads.'

I gasped and Hindley laughed. I hit his arm.

'No, they are just wearing normal stuff, like a black shirt

and black pants. Then, when they are convinced you are ready, you expose your neck and they take blood from you with their teeth, and then you get to do the same to them.' He looked around. 'It's bizarre at first but the rush you get when that blood hits you is unbelievable.'

'No regrets?' I asked.

'Hell no. You should see and smell and feel how I'm feeling. It's like everything is high powered. It's unreal,' he said. 'I wish Mum and Dad had done it.'

It was the first time Hindley had ever said that; he hadn't been close to Dad over the last few years and I wasn't sure he even missed them.

'Me too. It'd be great to have them around forever.'

We sat in silence for a few moments, and then he turned to face me. 'I've got to tell you something, about your dickhead adopted brother.'

I frowned at Hindley. 'He's got a name.'

'Yeah.' He ignored that suggestion. 'Have you seen him since he came back?'

'He came by earlier this week. We haven't really spoken though, I kind of threw him out,' I said and shrugged. I didn't like to give Hindley ammunition for liking Heath even less, but it was the truth.

'Good. Keep that up,' he said and looked happy. 'It'd be great if you and Edgar were on, great for business too. Plus, you are suited – you're both quiet and classy, not moody like dickhead.'

I gave him a smirk this time. 'So, what do you have to tell me?' I reminded him.

‘Oh yeah.’ He ran his hand through his hair and looked out at the surrounding landscape before answering. It was like he was looking for something; I followed his gaze but saw nothing but the hills.

Hindley looked straight at me and said in the most serious voice I’ve ever heard him use, especially as he normally didn’t seem to care what I did: ‘I want you to be careful around him.’

‘Why?’ I asked, worried. ‘What’s he done?’

‘He’s found his heritage and it’s not what—’

Just as he was about to explain, a dozen party-goers hammered down the front stairs towards us, including Dan, Sean and Tilly. The door remained open, and the music followed them out. We stood up to save being trampled on.

‘Where have you been, bro?’ Dan asked, pulling Hindley close to him. ‘Come on, we’re about to clear out of here and head into town. The youngies are staying on for a while,’ he said, with a nod to most of the under-agers, like Tilly and me!

I looked to Hindley and he mouthed the words, ‘tell you later.’

I glanced at my watch and it was nearly one in the morning. Tilly got my meaning, she had a 1.30am curfew.

‘We’ve got to go,’ she said, and Sean looked disappointed. ‘Curfew,’ Tilly explained.

‘Right, been there, had that. Let’s swap numbers,’ Sean said, and grabbing his phone out of his pocket, he handed it to Tilly, who smiled and happily put her number in. Sean rang it and Tilly’s phone rang in her handbag.

'Now you've got me,' he said.

So cute, those two, hope it becomes something. While they were saying goodbye, I grabbed Dan and planted a kiss on his glowing cheek. He always had nice blue eyes but now they were amazing, you just wanted them to focus on you.

'Hey thanks for the invite, it was a great party,' I said, 'and by the way, you look *soooo* good.'

He grinned and wrapped me in a hug before the others pulled him away.

Tilly linked her arm in mine and we made our way to her car. She talked about Sean all the way there, all the way home, and I think she was still talking about him after I exited the car… I don't think she noticed I'd gone! Ah, love.

I just realised I'd had fun. For the first time in a year, I laughed, danced, didn't have to worry that Heath was dead and didn't think about Heath or Edgar, much.

I turned around and wasn't alone.

A dark figure was standing there in the shadows.

Chapter 16 – Introduction to a hybrid

Catherine

I gasped in fright. It was dark, the wind's song was low and deep, and the figure stepped out of the shadows.

Heath held up his hands. 'Sorry, I didn't mean to scare you.'

'How could you not?' I said, breathing fast. 'I'm here alone and you step out of the shadows!'

We stared at each other for a moment. He looked like everything I wanted standing there waiting for me. I wanted to run to him and hold him and just feel good again, but I was so angry that my feet were rooted to the spot.

'I need to talk with you, Cathy.'

I began to speak, and he cut me off.

'I will explain what has happened and why I left and then I'll leave you to process it,' he said it with finality like it was a foregone conclusion and there was to be no argument on the subject. 'When you are ready, I'll come back for you.'

'Ha, will you now?' I scoffed. Perhaps he shouldn't have added that last statement, he had me until then. I straightened. 'You don't get to order me around, Heath. You're only two years older than me, you're not my father or my brother, in fact, we're not even related.'

'Oh, we're family, Cathy. We might not be blood siblings, but we're family and we will be for life.'

He stood there full of entitlement, as if I were his property. He had changed in that year he was away; he was stronger, more confident in himself.

Then I realised what it was, he didn't need us anymore. Sure, he wanted me, but he didn't need the Earnshaws anymore. Everything about this house was his history and the only connection to it was me. He didn't have to come home because Dad was gone and there was no loyalty to repay. But worse, he hated Hindley with a passion that has grown for years and this house reminded him of that.

'Where are you staying?' I asked. 'Have you got your own place now?'

'Nothing permanent. I'm at Dane's place, near the winery,' he said.

I knew the place well, they were new apartments with great views of the moors, the village, and our vineyards.

'Let's go inside,' he said.

I took a deep breath and he watched me, waiting for my response.

'Do you know anything about that killing, the druggy?' I asked him. I didn't want to know the answer, but I had to ask.

'I didn't do it if that's what you are asking.' He turned away, avoiding my eyes like he was hiding something.

'I never thought you did.'

'Really?' he caught my eye.

'Never.' I studied him. 'But you know something… you know who did, don't you?'

He gave just the slightest nod. Holy crap! Then something flew out of the tree and startled me, and even Heath jumped.

'Let's go to your room and talk,' he said again. He sensed my hesitation. 'Please Cathy, hear me out and then I'll leave.'

I still hoped he would tell me some story that made all the last year excusable. I shivered with the cold and he slipped his coat jacket off for me. I rejected it and walked to the front door. He followed. I guess it was worth a try on his behalf since I didn't out and out tell him to get lost.

Nelly had left on a light for me downstairs, and I unlocked the front door and we entered. I asked him would he like a drink. I hate I was so polite when I was busy trying to hate him. He declined and reached for my hand, catching me unaware. Then he led me up the stairs to my room. It was in darkness with just a sliver of moonlight shining through the windows; the fingers of the branches were shadow dancing across the ceiling. I pulled my hand out of his, but I didn't turn on the light, nor did Heath.

I dropped my bag on the chair in the corner and watched as he slipped his jacket over the back of the chair. Heath went to the window and leaning against the frame, looked out. He scanned the moors as if looking for something. I lowered myself on the end of the bed and waited for him to speak.

'I didn't leave because I stopped loving you,' he said and turned to face me. 'I left because I loved you and I wanted you to see me as something more than the dirty, orphaned kid your family had given charity to all those years.'

'I never—'

He cut me off. 'How could you not? Somewhere in your psyche, you know that I'd be probably living on the streets if your dad hadn't brought me home. All those years your brother treated me like the hired help. And…' he swallowed, and turned to look back out the window, 'I heard what you said to Nelly and I understand that.'

'You took it out of context,' I said in a low voice. I was ashamed that he heard my words. 'I never said you weren't good enough. I'd never think like that. It's just you and I are all we've ever known. Haven't you ever looked at anyone else at school and thought it might be fun to take them out? Don't you worry that in a decade or more we'll look at each other and think we've missed out on something?'

Heath gave a bitter laugh. 'In that entire school, Cathy, not one person ever came close to you for me. Every day I'm not with you I hate what I've missed out on. So no, I don't feel that and I won't feel like that in ten years or a hundred years. But you needed more.'

I groaned and put my head in my hand; I loved his words, it's just what I needed to hear but then why leave me without a word? I swallowed, remembering what I said and how, out of context, it must have wounded him. I looked up at him. His expression said he didn't trust the words I was saying now.

'That's why you left?' I asked. 'Just because you overheard that? You could have talked with me,' I said.

'You know I've felt for so long that I didn't belong here, that I was lucky, that I had to be grateful, and plenty of people told me that over the years too,' Heath said. 'Never you though, I never heard that from you until then. Until you thought that there might be something better for you out there.'

We fell into silence; I could hear the wind moaning.

Eventually, he continued. 'It's ironic, I guess, because I thought you were the gift given to me to make up for my parents abandoning me and being seen as the orphaned kid. I could put up with Hindley and worse, just to be near you every day, Cathy.'

I bit back tears; I knew I had played a part in it but I didn't realise the load he was carrying.

'I had to stand on my own and make something of myself so that you would see me differently,' he said. 'I didn't expect to find out where I came from, but I wanted to give you the space to miss me and to think about what you wanted and to grow without my influence. I wanted to be sure of what I wanted too, and not just hang around the business working at it because Dad gave it to us on a plate.'

I stood up and came closer to him, leaning on the other side of the windowsill.

'I could live with all that,' I said, 'if you had just sent me some word that you were okay and that you'd be back some day.'

'But then you would have waited for me. Which kind of defeats the purpose of what I thought we both needed to go through, or at least what you told Nelly you needed.'

I thought about his words, but I still didn't buy it. If I knew he was off doing his own thing and safe, I might have done the same. 'Well it worked,' I said. 'I'm with Edgar now.' I knew it was cruel to say it but I was still smarting from a year's worth of pain.

His eyes flared with anger. 'How long have you been with him?'

'Not long. Does it matter?'

'Has he touched you?'

I didn't answer and his jaw tightened as he glared out the window. Then I saw it in his anger. A flare of yellow in his eyes, and I gasped and stepped back.

'Heath!'

He turned to me, his face flashing with fear, anger, power.

'What are you?'

*****

Heath

I saw the fear in her face, and I saw something else too... a look I knew well. I'm not pure bred, I'm a mixed breed, a hybrid. Always just not quite good enough.

'It's okay,' I said, and moved towards her, but she stepped back in fear, so I retreated. I rushed to tell her my story in case she didn't give me the chance.

'I returned to London, to the area that my family dumped me in as a kid. I had a hazy memory of it, but in all honesty, I didn't expect to find it or to find that the landmarks I remembered would be there, but they were.'

She was staying with me. Cautious, but attentive. I swallowed and continued; I haven't spoken this much in a year.

'I asked around if anyone remembers a rich white guy coming into the area and offering to look after a kid, aged about eight, and taking him away with him.' I shrugged. 'It was over a decade ago and a long shot, but there were a few market stall holders who had been in the area a lot longer than that, and they saw everything. One older couple were good people, they wouldn't accept anything from me for the information – money, dinner, goods. They had pride.'

I saw her face softening as I wove the story.

'They remembered not only your dad, but me, and they remembered what happened to my parents. They gave me the name of someone who witnessed the entire event. It took a lot of digging but eventually, the truth came out. I guess like our culture, your culture, no one is too keen to share stories of hybrids with strangers asking questions.'

'Hybrid,' Cathy said the word with caution, as though it would summon more. 'What does it mean? I've never met a hybrid.'

'My parents were murdered, shunned by their family and communities. My mother was a vampire from a very well-to-do London-based family and she fell in love with my father, a werewolf from an ancient British family. Both families forbid the mixed relationship. After they conceived me, my mother had her Conversion to ensure her safety, but it wasn't enough. They were exiled and murdered.'

Cathy gasped and put her hands up to her face. So beautiful and compassionate, my Cathy.

'Your father knew my mother's family and was angered by their actions. He came looking for me; I was unwanted by both sides and was surviving on the streets. He rescued me and brought me here, to Wuthering Heights.'

'He's such a good man,' she said.

'He always was a man of integrity,' I said. 'I am the only survivor of that union. I am the only descendant of my mother's family and I am legally a very wealthy man, Cathy. We'll never want for anything, no matter what Hindley does to the business.'

She was standing there stunned, her face was pale and I thought she was going to faint.

I reached out my hand for her, but she lowered herself on the edge of her bed. I could sense she was very wary of me now.

'What does it mean for you though, Heath? A hybrid? Will you be weaker?'

'Oh no, Cathy, just the opposite,' I said, and gave her an assuring smile. 'I've inherited powers of both vampires and werewolves so I am not only incredibly powerful, but I heal super fast and my blood can heal you. The sun and moon do not affect me and I can change at any time, not just when the moon has its way. And if I have my way, Cathy, you will accept me as I am… it's a new generation, we don't have to be exiled for being different. Look at mum and dad, your parents,' I clarified, 'they chose not to have the Conversion, we can choose to live as a vampire and hybrid. Times have changed, we won't be shunned.'

She was studying me like she hadn't known me most of her life, like I was a completely new creature to her.

I reached for her and she allowed me to hold it this time; it was cold, she was pale and I knew she had a lot going through her head. I kissed her hand and I heard her make a small sound, a desperate sound of despair that resonated through me. I give her a small bow and then I left.

I heard her words as I departed: 'Show me.'

Chapter 17 – What to do

Catherine

After Heath left it poured. The rain tapped on the windows like morse code telling me to forgive him, make a decision, make the right one, whatever that was. The wind howled and shadows whipped around the room like frenzied fingers reaching for me.

I sat on the edge of my bed, frozen. What do I do with this… this larger than life, life-changing, bigger than all of us news that Heath just dumped on me? When he was talking, I was trying so hard to focus on him and not how much I wanted to hold him and have him hold me. Now this. I dropped back on my bed and stared at the ceiling.

I desperately wanted to believe he didn't kill that man, but he now belongs to two families – the werewolf clan and our vampire culture. He was always torn as a kid and now it just goes on, he's torn between two clans. And he's found wealth, I can't believe it. He's so different. My Dad was so good to bring Heath home. If it hadn't been for Hindley, perhaps Heath's remaining childhood could have been good. What a miserable time he had of it.

I don't know how I feel about him testing me to see if I'd stray and testing my feelings for him. Why doesn't he stay and prove his love for me? Come back home and be here with me. Kiss me like a lover, like a boyfriend, not like siblings or friends who have always been in each other's orbits.

I have to find him tonight. I want to see him, the real him. I want to know every detail of the last year of his life and I want to know how he feels about us. I wouldn't sleep tonight without speaking with him again. I grabbed my phone and rang him; it went to his message bank. I paced, so frustrated, feeling so much turmoil that I couldn't believe the atmosphere didn't reflect it. I rang him again, no answer. I changed quickly, putting on my runners, jeans and a pullover, a baseball cap, plus my weatherproof jacket. I grabbed my umbrella for what use it would be in this wind and headed down the stairs. It was stupid to go out in this weather, this late, but I couldn't stay in that room a minute longer. The room and the house were suffocating me. I had to find Heath and get answers.

It was good to be out walking, to feel something even if it was wet and cold, to be doing something other than waiting, which I've been doing all year. Moving as fast as I could, I headed down the driveway and tucked my hands deep into my coat, my umbrella hanging from the crook in my arm. The road was wide and well-marked for the tourist traffic, but there were no cars around, and it was only dimly lit by moonlight. The rain had eased up, but every shadow looked sinister and every sound was a wild animal.

I am so stupid doing this, I scolded myself, but I couldn't go back now. I just kept walking as fast as I could. Eventually, I came to the edge of the village and I saw the hall where we'd partied earlier. There were still a few partygoers scattered on the stairs, drinking and talking. They couldn't see me in the dark fringe of the road. The winery was just past this turn and not much further over the moors. I knew the cut through like the back of my hand; I could have done it blindfolded for the number of times I had taken this route every day over the years to school, to sport, to dance, to parties. Tonight, I'd be taking it to Heath.

I left the main road and headed across the low rises. It was boggy from the wet, but I knew the best paths to take. I passed a small waterfall that I loved, I loved the sound of it and sitting here in summer was so peaceful. Heath and I would ride our horses here when we were kids and sit on the rocks with our feet in the cold water. Heath, Heath, Heath, everything reminded me of him.

The wind was rising, and a chill was moving in. I hoped it wouldn't fog over before I got across the moors. I heard a low howl and the hairs on the back of my neck stood up. I looked around. I couldn't see anything or anyone, but then I couldn't see much of anything. The higher I walked towards the winery and Heath's place in the village, the more the fog descended. Maybe I shouldn't have taken the shortcut; I turned around and could see behind me clearly, but ahead it was misty. My feet found the rocks that I knew so well and I pushed on.

You're an idiot, you should be at home warm and safe in

bed, I told myself, but I still couldn't go back home. I should have gone on to the club with Hindley and Dan, stayed out until I was too tired to think.

I froze, I heard a sound, a rustling near me. I grabbed my umbrella and held it out like a weapon – I guess it would have looked pretty funny to anyone watching me. I narrowed my eyes trying to see ahead, but I could only see a few meters in front of me. I was breathing fast and I kept thinking of the murdered body found last week; the killer was still out there. I looked behind and considered turning back, but I'd come so far now that I was closer to the winery and Aden's place – where Heath was staying – than I was to the road.

I kept thinking what the people of The Moors would say the next day – the people from the village. They'd say I was lost since my parents died, that I wandered out in despair. They'll secretly think what a silly young woman I was wandering around in the dark. They'll blame Nelly and Heath and Hindley for not stepping up for me when it is all my fault. What was I thinking? I waited but heard nothing more; I lowered my umbrella and continued. The fog was thickening, I could see less and less. The moors were always so unpredictable, but now I was the one caught in the dark and the fog – the very thing we warn the tourists about.

Something touched me in the fog and I reeled around. There was no one there. Was it Hindley and Daniel being stupid or hunting in their new vampire state?

I called out Hindley's name.

'You're scaring me, please stop it,' I cried. He might be a

smart arse at times, but he would not continue if he knew I was frightened.

I felt something touch my back and spun. No one was there. Then fingers brushed my arm, I wheeled around, all I could see was fog and then I heard a deep laugh.

I stumbled forward, disorientated. Which way was I going? The fog was too thick to tell. How did this happen? I knew this way, this journey was my own, my life. Which way do I go?

I felt someone right near me again, hot breath and a growl, and I screamed. Then I felt the impact; something hit my shoulder and I lost my balance and hit the ground hard. I covered my face with my hands; I didn't want to look. The knock was so hard that I couldn't get my breath.

Suddenly there was a roar and the air filled with powerful energy. I saw swift movements and yelling and I cowered, staying low.

I felt powerful arms lifting me and wrapping around me and I struck out, fighting back, scared to open my eyes.

'Cathy, Cathy, stop, it's me, you 're safe.'

I knew the voice. Heath. I opened my eyes and tears streamed down my face. I knew I was shaking and not just from the cold.

He held me closer. 'What are you doing here?'

'I wanted to see you, I needed to see you,' I cried. 'What happened? What was that?' I looked around as much as I could while pressed to his chest. The wind was merciless and the fog moved in around us.

He shushed me. 'I don't know. Something, someone was

following you. I ran at them and for a moment we fought but then they took off.'

'Did you injure them? It?' I asked.

'I don't know, but you're safe.' He kept walking and carrying me like I was weightless. I leaned against him. He was warm and strong, safe, and I was drained.

'I would have come to you, you just had to call,' Heath said.

'I couldn't stay at home any longer. You left, again,' I said, between tearful gulps. 'I needed to see you.'

He kissed the top of my head. 'I'm sorry, Cathy, I'm not very good at this.'

'At what?'

'At being at odds with you. I don't know how to fix it,' he said with raw honesty.

He walked fast, not looking back until his place came into sight. Heath started up the stairs, opened the door and carried me straight through to a bedroom, kicking the door closed behind him. He placed me on my feet, removed my jacket, and sat me on the bed as he took off my runners and wet socks. He lay me back on his bed as he removed his jacket and shoes. He lay next to me and enveloped me in his arms; his body warmth working wonders for me.

I closed my eyes in relief and offered a silent prayer of thanks; I didn't think I would get here. I honestly thought I'd be a statistic in the morning press. Some tragic kid who goes down in folklore and the next generation of schoolies my age visits my grave and tells ghost stories. Yeah, I think way too much.

Heath looked down at me; he brushed the wet hair from my face and brought me back to the now.

'You're shaking, let's get you to a warm shower and into some drier clothes,' he said, rising.

I stopped him and touched his cheek with my hand. He clenched his jaw and closed his eyes, reigning in his emotions. It was the first time we had touched in over a year, except for the quick kiss he had delivered to my hand earlier tonight, which felt like a hundred years ago.

'Please, can we just lie here?'

He nodded.

'How did you know to come to me?' I asked him.

He looked uncomfortable.

'No, Heath! You were following me… it was you that scared me?' I asked incredulously and pulled away from him. 'I was so terrified!'

'No, never. I would never, ever do that, Cathy.' He cleared his throat. 'I could smell you.'

I sat up on my elbows. 'What do you mean?' *How horrifying. Did I stink?*

'I always had heightened smell, even as a kid, but I never understood why. The older I got, the stronger it got; now I know why. I could smell you nearby,' he said, with a shrug. 'I was out on the balcony having a drink, thinking about our discussion, and I caught your scent. I thought I was imagining it, but it didn't go away and then I heard you yell. It's the wolf side of me – my hearing and smell senses are amazing.'

I was still a bit horrified, even if I was relieved that he caught my scent and rescued me.

‘What do I smell like?’ I asked. I only wanted to know if it was good.

He smiled. ‘Beautiful.’

I think I reddened with relief. ‘Thank you, but really,’ I asked, ‘what can you smell?’

He took my hand from his cheek and kissed inside, on my palm. He ran his fingers over my palm and goosebumps broke out all over me.

‘Talcum powder, wild lavender, and fear,’ he said.

I sighed. I always wore talcum powder. I know it was old-fashioned but I loved it on my body after a shower, and my perfume was English Lavender. Way uncool but my grandmother and mother wore it, and it was comforting, a classic.

‘That’s me – wildflower and scaredy-cat,’ I said, summing up my scent.

‘Feminine, graceful,’ he said, looking into my eyes. I desperately wanted him to kiss me. Why didn’t he try to kiss me?

I turned away. ‘Thank you,’ I said, too exhausted to move now that I was safe and there were only a few hours until dawn broke.

Heath drew me closer; I rested my head on his chest.

‘You were crazy being out so late, next time call me,’ he scolded.

‘I wanted the walk; besides you and I know every step on that walk,’ I said, mumbling now that I was slowing down into sleep.

‘Well, we’re not the only ones out there anymore,’ he reminded me.

‘Heath?’ I turned my face to him. Here goes. ‘I want you to kiss me.’

He froze and he studied me like he wanted to do a lot more than that. I think he wanted to swallow me whole.

He shook his head. ‘Our first passionate kiss will not be on one of the worst nights of your life… that’d be bad karma and a shit memory.’

I pouted, and he chuckled.

‘You’re hard work, Ms Earnshaw.’

‘I am not,’ I said indignantly. I would have given him a good slap on the arm for that if I had the energy. ‘I have questions I need to ask you.’

‘Ask me in the morning. I’ll answer them all,’ he assured me in a soothing voice.

And we slept. My last conscious thought was that somewhere, outside, an evil presence still roamed free, but I was safe in Heath’s arms.

Chapter 18 – High Society

Catherine

It was early, just after seven, and we'd only been asleep a few hours; I heard Heath moving around, getting dressed. He had showered and looked gorgeous and comfortable with his unfamiliar look – dress pants, a T-shirt and a suit jacket. He came back and sat on the edge of the bed. I didn't have Heath's sensory strengths yet, but I could smell his sensual cologne on the pillow.

'Why are you up so early? It's Saturday,' I said, stretching out across both sides of the bed.

'I've got to go to work, Conrad's meeting me there at eight. It's a new business,' he said. 'By the way, I rang Nelly and told her you were safe.' He touched my face with his hand.

'Are you alright?' he asked.

'I think so. I kept waking every time I thought about what might have happened if you hadn't been there.'

'I'll always be there. Come on, I'll drop you home before my meeting.' He rose and pulled the curtains open. It was a great apartment. The views of the moors and village were fantastic and private given Heath, or Aden's loft was on the top floor.

I raised myself on one elbow; clearly, that was a subtle hint to get up and get dressed.

'You promised to answer my questions this morning – where you have been for the last year, who you met, what you know about your family, and what's the new business you've got… and us,' I said, pushing back the covers and getting out of bed. Half-dressed from last night, except for my boots and jacket, I brushed myself down like the creases would just vanish.

'We'll talk about us for sure,' he said. 'And I'll tell you in great detail tonight.'

Tonight. Uh oh, this was going to get ugly. He turned to look at me when I didn't respond. I grimaced.

'I've got plans for tonight.'

'Right,' he said. 'With whom?'

I hesitated, it's not like it was any of his business.

'Edgar,' I answered. 'I've got a date with Edgar.'

I felt the wall of cold hit me from where I was standing. Heath clenched his hands, his jaw locked and I swear his eyes would have flared red if that was possible. I lowered my eyes and focussed on putting my boots back on.

'Last night you wanted me to kiss you and yet you're still going to see him?' he asked in a very restrained voice.

'I… yes, it's arranged, and you didn't kiss me. Edgar and I set this up last week when you were only just back on the scene. Besides, I like Edgar, he's lovely.' I rose to full height and reached for my bag. In a flash, Heath was by my side, holding both of my arms and glaring down at me.

'Cathy, why would you do that to us?'

I looked at him incredulously. 'Heath, you've been back for a minute and you expect me to drop my plans and pick up where we left off? I don't even know how you feel about me or us. That's what I want to talk about, but you've blown that off again.' I pulled out of his arms and strode to the bedroom door.

He was there before I'd barely opened it, slamming it closed and pressing into me.

'Cathy, I've come back for you. I've come back a better man, worthy of you,' he said, close to my ear.

I slipped under his arm and turned to face him.

'Every waking moment I thought about you. I looked out for you in every crowd. I raced home after school in case you had returned. I went to our place on the moors and sat there for hours on end every weekend, just in case you came. I watched the moors change with the different light during the day, knowing how you loved that. I'd feel like the trees were swaying for me, feeling my anxiety. I'd feel guilty if I laughed or went to a dance because you might need me, be lost or in pain. By abandoning me without a word, all you did was guarantee you would be my focus for that whole time. And you were.'

Heath groaned and reached for me again. I shoved him away and I kept talking, the words poured out of me – a year's worth of anger.

'After a while, Heath, I wondered if you would ever come

back. I then started worrying that maybe you and Hindley had got into a fight and it had ended in death, and Hindley was just telling me you'd left when really you were dead and buried under the ground somewhere....' My voice broke and he ran his hand over his mouth. He could never stand it when I was upset.

I continued. 'So thinking you might be dead, then I really couldn't laugh or enjoy myself because what if your body was lying cold somewhere and I'm off having a good time. I couldn't feel you,' I told him. 'I thought you must be dead, because I had no sense of you at all. Then just before you reappear, Edgar asks me out and for the first time in a year, I let myself feel a bit happy. I had something to look forward to, and then in you rock ready to resume where we were. So no, Heath. No, I'm not calling off the date.'

He grabbed my hand. 'Cathy, everything you went through, I went through worse. I thought you wanted to try life without me. You don't know how that hit me, those words you said to Nelly... you are the only solid ground I have and then it shifted. All year I stayed busy trying not to think about what you were doing every minute of the day, or the guys that were asking you out, who you might flirt with, kiss, share your life with.' He swallowed. 'It was like bile constantly rising in my throat. I felt like everything had shifted – we were no longer looking at the same sky or standing on the same earth. So don't tell me about your anguish, you put this into action – you caused this pain to both of us.'

We both glared at each other. And then he drew a deep breath.

'Let's go, I'll drop you home,' he said again and turned back to the table near his bed, grabbed his keys and wallet and headed for the door. I stopped him.

'Heath, stop, please.'

He turned to face me, masking all emotions.

'You didn't hear everything I said to Nelly that day or you would have never left.' I put my hand on his chest and felt the heat near his heart. 'You are more myself than I am. We are meant to be.'

'And yet you will go to the boy you are *fond* of,' he said, and opening the door, walked out.

I followed.

*****

Going to Edgar's place was like stepping into another time. My home was sparse on luxuries, it was practical and modern, with minimalist furniture – a reflection of my parents. They made us participate in the home and farm chores, to work in the business, and to earn our own pocket money. Dad was big on instilling a healthy survival and real-world edge in us. However, Edgar's home was just the opposite. It was luscious – full of chandeliers and luxuries, plush rugs and paintings. It was like I came from a sparse modern art gallery into a classic antique store – very upmarket. And that's what Edgar's family was like, too. His mother looked like she just stepped out of a beauty salon, his father was so pristine that sometimes I thought he was a mannequin model, and Isabella was sweet and pretty and scarily innocent. I hope she's ready for the world out there, which is nothing like the home she lives in.

I did my best to dress as if I belonged in their world – a pale pink twin set and matching skirt and colour coordinated shoes – yep, you could barely distinguish me from the furniture! And Edgar looked so pleased when he saw me, he really was gorgeous – handsome, sophisticated. I was different when I was with him.

After greeting his parents, accepting a drink, and making some polite small talk, they left us in the beautiful sunroom – that's what they called it – and Edgar put some music on.

'You look beautiful, Cathy,' he said.

He always made me blush, as if I'd never had a compliment before. We sat opposite each other on a cosy chaise lounge and his hand touched my shoulder. Then I saw the newspaper on the table in front of us.

'Oh my God, have you seen this I ask?' leaning forward and grabbing it.

The headline read: *A Vigilante in The Moors.*

I read through the story. It was what happened last night on the moors, where I was.

Police believe they are now searching for a vigilante after the second death of two men with criminal records in The Moors' Village within a week. The body of a man, aged 32, known to police from former domestic violence charges, was found last night on the moors approximately 1.5 kilometres from the main road. The man had been viciously attacked and died at the scene. Police are withholding his name until relatives are notified. The death earlier this week of a known drug dealer had strong similarities according to police. A police media spokesperson said a press conference would be held later today but police have reiterated that people should not take justice into their own hands but use the resources of their local constabulary.

I had temporarily forgotten Edgar was there, and I looked up to find him watching me.

'Do you know something about this?' he asked, leaning forward.

I nodded and sat back, turning to face him. 'I was at a 21st party last night and I went for a walk after,' I said, leaving out some details. 'I was on the moors when I thought I heard something.'

Edgar gasped. 'Whoever it was could have killed you, Cathy. You shouldn't be out alone, especially out there alone.'

'I know, I was stupid,' I agreed.

'What did you hear? A scream?' Edgar asked.

I shook my head. 'More of a fight, but I couldn't see anything in the fog. I just heard the sounds of fighting.'

He groaned. Everyone who lives in The Moors knows how the fog moves in quickly and for the unsuspecting, it is really dangerous. Deaths had been recorded in the past from people who got disorientated and lost, then fallen to their death or drowned in the cold creeks and rivers.

I continued. 'You know how quiet it is on the moors at night, the fight could have been further away and the sound just travelling,' I said, with a shrug, trying to salvage my reputation so Edgar didn't think I was a total idiot wandering around at night aimlessly.

'I can't believe you were out there, walking alone at night,' he said, and took my hands. 'Promise me, Cathy, if you get stuck or need a ride, you'll call me anytime. I mean it, anytime. I'll come.' He looked at me so sincerely that I found myself studying his face, and then I realised he was leaning in and his lips touched mine. He moved closer and reached for me. It felt so good, so romantic in this room filled with light.

Then I realised he was my first ever real romantic kiss. It should have been Heath.

*****

Loud laughter followed by Isabella and Jace interrupted our kissing as they crashed in. So Jace was in and Heath was off the scene? She reddened when she saw me, like she was betraying Heath. Yep, we both felt that way. So great to see Jace with her, he gave me a look that said 'winner'.

'Sorry,' Isabella said, 'are we interrupting?'

'Yes,' her brother said, and we all laughed, even though he wasn't joking. Remembering his manners – oh so cultured – he rose and retracted the remark.

'Not at all. Hi Jason,' he said, and they shook hands. 'I remember you from school, well the footy team, you were good.'

'Thanks.' Jace shrugged. 'I was just a fast runner, more to the point, so if I held the ball while I was going in one direction, I looked like I could play.'

We all laughed again. Very chilled.

'Not true, you are talented,' I told him, then reined it in. I remembered Tilly telling me that Jace likes me. Don't want to appear flirty in front of his 'date' or mine.

'Join us if you like,' Edgar said, although I don't think he really wanted them to. Bad luck, they did. It relieved my anxiety since I was still working out the Heath versus Edgar, torn between two lovers thing.

They sat nearby and worked their way through Mr Linton's vinyl collection.

'So cool,' Jace said, sitting right beside Isabella and checking out the album covers.

I knew Mr and Mrs Linton would never be rude, but Jace would not be there first or the last choice for Isabella. He wasn't from our blood strain... she'd have to convert him or not convert herself and that's fraught with danger where his relatives are concerned. But hey, they're just hanging out, let's not read too much into it.

Edgar went to get more drinks and some chips and dips. We had fun. It was the first relaxed, chilled afternoon I'd had with friends in a long time where I wasn't stressing out, worried or going over too many things in my head. My life with Edgar would be so different from a life with HeatI felt at home.

I didn't know that Heath, in his other form, was watching me.

Chapter 19 - Vigilante

Heath

The rage was roaring through my body with such ferocity that I could feel all my nerve endings on alert. My Cathy kissed that anaemic guy in his bland, posh house – sitting on that couch as if she belonged there. The four of them, socialising in a world that I'd never be let into or feel part of. Is that seriously what she wants?

I let the anger overtake me for the second time. This time the conversion felt healing instead of terrifying. The sharp pain of adjustment was consoling. I needed to feel it, to funnel my rage somewhere. Then I ran in my wolf's form as fast and as far away from them as my shape would allow. Across the moors, through the long grasses, over the valleys, across the rocks, through creeks, until I couldn't run anymore and I collapsed on the ground in exhaustion.

My limbs ached, I panted and sucked in as much air as I could, and my heart ached. I've lost her, I know I have. She's gone to him and that lifestyle. Cathy will never fit in there, she's just caught up in the gloss and the glamour.

Edgar thinks she's a lady who will entertain and be content to share his smiles. He needs to scratch the surface to find the real girl. Cathy is as wild as I am, it's in her blood and she and I both know it. She's a little spoilt, a tomboy, and dressing up to play ladies won't last for long; she needs to run away to the moors and have time out to be herself. She'll never survive if she has to display social graces around the clock. I scoffed at the thought – I would almost like to see if she could pull it off, but I know she'd be miserable. Will she be miserable without me though?

*****

Catherine

I was going to get a lift home with Jace and his mum when she arrived to pick him up – it will be so much better when we get our licences – but Edgar asked me to stay, and promised to drop me home afterwards.

'I want to show you something, but I had to wait until nightfall,' he said as we left Isabella and Jace to say their farewells. He read my expression and laughed. 'It's perfectly legitimate,' he said and rolled his eyes.

I grinned. 'You're not the first guy that's offered to show me something,' I teased.

'Come on.' He extended his hand, and I put mine in his. So smooth and sexy. Then he led me through the house to the far wing, which was pretty much just a couple of empty big rooms.

‘It’s for functions,’ he explained. ‘When Mum does her fundraising stuff, they have the lunches or balls in here. It’s got a private entrance and car park,’ he said and nodded to the outside view.

‘Ah, makes sense,’ I agreed. He then opened a door and inside was a narrow staircase.

‘You go first in case you fall and I’ll be behind to catch you,’ he said, maybe gallantly. I gave him another suspicious look and he laughed again.

‘Wow, you’ve got us guys all worked out,’ he said.

‘I have brothers,’ I said without thinking. I really only had one blood brother and I was trying hard not to think about the other one, Heath. I took to the steps and after climbing the equivalent of two stories, I came to another door. Edgar could fit on the small landing next to me, he leaned into me and unlocked it, pushing it open.

We exited onto the roof of part of the house and it was like nothing I had ever seen. Huge big panel windows that were floor to ceiling and you could see out at the distance sky forever. Edgar flicked on some very low lights and in the centre was a telescope and some couches. In the corner were fridges stocked with drinks and glasses. Edgar took me over to the couch and offered me a seat. He then grabbed a remote and sat beside me. With the push of one button, he opened the roof to the world. Well, that’s what it felt like… like the entire night’s sky was on show for us. The roof panels slid into each other until the entire roof was glass to the edge of the glass windows.

I felt like I could see the universe, and the sky was clear

with hundreds and thousands of twinkling stars. He used the remote to turn off all the lights which made them shine even brighter.

'Oh my God, Edgar, this is breathtaking.'

'It's a beautiful show,' he agreed. 'I love it here.'

'Wow, makes you feel small though,' I said in a quiet voice, not wanting to disturb the peaceful atmosphere.

'I can open it right up, remove all the glass ceiling too. That's really something but it is chilly,' he said. 'Want to?'

'Absolutely,' I enthused.

'Okay, you'll need to move closer and I'll keep you warm.' He gave me an inviting grin and I laughed as I slid over on the leather couch and snuggled under his arm. He pressed a button and it began. It was like the sky opening for us… chilly, beautiful, quiet, a painting of sparkling diamonds across black velvet. And me, sitting with a beautiful man who was still and calm and in love with me.

Chapter 20 – Confronting love

Catherine

'O-M-G, Dad is so busy with this killer on the loose,' Tilly said as we walked down the hallway to art class. It was her favourite class because she topped it, and my favourite because I could relax in it and we got to talk while we created. Today was our last day of painting our self-portraits. We entered the room, greeted Ms Sumina, and set up our easels. Some of the self-portrait paintings were just brilliant. I looked at mine, it hadn't improved with age since last week.

'Do they have any leads,' I asked Tilly once we were at work.

'No, but Dad says the killings were violent,' she said lowering her voice and leaning into me. 'Torn throats, lots of blood on the ground, would have been quick at least.'

I grimaced as she told me. I know I was from a bloodline of vampires, but I had a weak stomach for violence. I'd never be able to be a doctor or nurse.

Ms Sumina was making her way around the class and arrived beside us.

'Oh Tilly, that really is something,' she said. 'You should hang it in your household once we finish the semester, I'm sure your parents will love it.'

Tilly grinned. 'Thanks, Ms Sumina. It's been fun.'

'What are you planning to do with your talent? Will you go on and study art?' she asked.

'I'd like to sketch for the police and courts, work with my father,' Tilly said. 'Some of the witness sketching and courtrooms scenes are amazing to do and they often appear in national media.'

I'm sure that's not what Ms Sumina had in mind for Tilly, but she was always supportive.

'Wow, well that's certainly different. Perhaps you could also do some of your own work with a view to having a showing at some point and time.'

She moved over to my work and, the poor woman, what can you say. I saved her from the trouble.

'I'm going to hang it in my house at Halloween,' I said, and Ms Sumina laughed. So did most of the class.

'Art comes in many forms, Cathy, well done,' she said, and moved away, probably silently saying a prayer and throwing some holy water over her shoulder hoping to excise the image of my painting from her memory. Okay, it's not that bad.

Tilly moved closer and continued talking about the killer. 'Even though Dad accepts this killer is a possible good guy vigilante, he doesn't want me going out at night until they have caught the person,' she said.

'Not at all?' I frowned, knowing we had a few parties

coming up. It would be a bummer to miss them and I wouldn't go without Tilly.

'He'll soften up if we're driven there and back,' she said. 'Are you scared?'

I thought about it. 'A little, but only because my house is so isolated. But I'd be more scared if they weren't calling him a vigilante and if he wasn't killing bad people.'

Tilly agreed. 'Whoever it is, they are super strong and very angry.'

Ms Sumina called for our attention and talked about some of the art world's most historic and recent famous self-portraits and I drifted away, thinking of the killer and thinking about Tilly's last words to me –*whoever it is, they are super strong and very angry.*

I knew a lot of super-strong people and a few that were angry at the world. Heath for starters. Did he have a bloodlust now with this other side of him – the werewolf side – coming through? My knowledge of werewolves was pretty much zilch. I'd have to get up to speed.

Then there was Hindley. He's just gone through the Conversion and he's pushing the boundaries on everything at the moment. Might he be tempted to hunt and to taste blood from a wild hunt, just once, or twice, as is the case here? Is Hindley justifying it by only killing what he always called scumbags? Our clan does it occasionally, who doesn't want to try it just for the speed and rush? But they hunt animals, not people, and authorities just blame a wild dog or wild boar – both smart, cunning and with the teeth to do the job.

Then there's Daniel, Hindley's friend who just had the Conversion too. Are they pack hunting together for fun? But there's been blood left at the scene so they're not draining the bodies. They might be too clever to do that as well, it would lead straight to suspicions of a mythical proportion!

Or was it just some crazy person? Hell knows there's been a few of those over the years living here and passing through. That would be more worrying.

Super strong and very angry. My heart suddenly ached for Heath, I missed him. I remembered the times in our childhood when Hindley was so cruel.

We had escaped the two of us and ran across the moors. The air was crisp and the moors were green for as far as the eye could see. I loved being here, my soul ached to be amongst it. We ran until Wuthering Heights was out of sight and then we both dropped behind several large boulders where we could look down over the rises, and see the waterfall, and see if anyone was coming.

Heath and I were both panting, but it felt wonderful. We sat close like we always did, but this time he winced.

'What's the matter,' I asked him.

'It's nothing,' he dismissed me. It wasn't nothing. I knew Hindley and Heath came to blows regularly and every chance he had Hindley thrashed Heath. Dad reprimanded him of course, but he wasn't there often – he was away for weeks at a time on the road.

I sat upright and tried to pull Heath's shirt back from his shoulder. He brushed my hand away. He had way too much pride and he was always so humiliated if Hindley beat him in front of me; but Hindley was always going to win, he was much bigger than Heath.

'Let me see and don't be silly,' I said, insisting. I gasped. His shoulder was black with bruising.

'Heath, you need to see a doctor. Come, we're going back and Nelly will call him.'

'We're not going back and we're not telling Nelly, it's nothing,' he said, and shrugged his shirt back up.

I watched him and he turned away from me.

'I hate him,' he hissed, 'and one day, Cathy, I will take my revenge on your brother.'

'Don't say that, Heath,' I scolded him, scared of the consequences. 'We have to learn to forgive and Nelly said God will punish those who deserve it.'

Heath shook his head. 'No. I bet God punishes many people. He won't get as much satisfaction out of punishing Hindley as I will. Sometimes it's the only thing that gets me through – planning what I'll do to him one day.'

I couldn't bear it when Heath and Hindley spoke like this. I lived in fear that one day it would end with one of them in the ground. Just last week I saw Hindley throw a heavy iron from his weight set at Heath hitting him in the chest. Heath didn't see it coming. Dad said if it happened again, he would send Hindley to boarding school. That made Hindley hate Heath even more if it was possible! I was terrified of the day when Dad and Mum might be away together; there's no way Nellie could restrain them and who knows what might happen. I was sick for thinking about it.

And Dad sent Hindley away to boarding school, so for a few years, Heath and I had peace. We roamed the moors, had so much freedom, and we spent a lot of time with Dad and Mum at the business. Dad really liked that and he liked Heath's keenness to learn everything he could. He'd wanted Hindley to show the same passion, but Hindley just wanted to see the balance sheet to find out how much money the business made. I can't imagine a world ever, where Hindley and Heath get on… the hatred is so deep-rooted.

Tilly had been talking to me and I missed what she said completely. Luckily she didn't stop to draw a breath, so I tried to catch up and nodded until I did. Does she know Jace was at Isabella's place on the weekend? Should I tell her? There needs to be a book on this sort of stuff… *What to Do in 50 Real-Life Situations.* Yeah, I'm liking that, I might write it myself.

'So do you want to?' Tilly asked.

Oh God, I've missed what she said again.

*****

Edgar

There were three interesting pieces of news when I arrived at work this morning. The first piece was that the police had no lead on the vigilante, allegedly, and the public was pleased about it according to a poll the paper took. Don't know who they polled or how many, but no one wanted the vigilante caught or punished, and parents were telling their kids that if they weren't good people, the vigilante would come for them too. Sigh, and I thought our culture was scary. The only downside was when we got their dead bodies on the slab, we couldn't milk much blood out of them. Not good for business, this vigilante.

The second piece of news is that the recently murdered guy, the one who beat up his wife, or so they say, was connected to our business. His wife, Melanie, works for us. She's a Sap and works in the funeral business, she's very sweet, compassionate and clients love her. Melanie is in her mid-thirties and we knew things weren't good on her home front. She'd show up with the tell-tale bruises and say she was clumsy; or with a black eye and say she ran into the cupboard or wall – a wall called her husband more like it. We all wanted to do something about it and we'd discussed it but they had children, she loved him or depended on him – it was complicated. When I found out it was her husband who was murdered, I wondered if any of our team would be capable of it.

Dad delivered the third interesting piece of news as I joined him and our small team in his office.

'I just received this by courier,' he said, holding up a letter. 'Hindley believes we're stalling and wants a decision on the profit percentage break by the end of this week.'

None of us could believe it. If we didn't have an option in the form of Heath's blood bank, would we have had to consider some action against Hindley… some violent action? It's not our scene but sometimes if called for, then so be it.

'We either reduce our profit or go elsewhere,' Dad concluded, raising his voice against the din of our disbelief.

'I suggest we have a good hard look at the Blood Banks' proposal ASAP,' Karl said.

I turned to our Director of Marketing. 'I suggest we back up all the databases today, just in case.'

'Good idea, today, definitely,' Dad agreed. We shared these databases of all the clients who bought blood and had it delivered to them. Two could play at Hindley's game, and if we did part ways, he would not leave us without our resources, namely our clients.

I couldn't help but wonder where the hell he was going to get his blood if he broke ties with us, or was he just that arrogant that he thought we had no options and we'd pay up?

*****

Catherine

Nelly and I were having dinner; she made a killer vegetarian lasagne and now there were only two of us to eat it.

'Have you seen him, Heath?' Nelly asked.

I shook my head. 'Not since after the party the other night. I thought he might have come over yesterday after I came back from Edgar's place,' I said, and sighed. 'I just think if he was missing me and wanting me as he says, he'd show up occasionally.'

'Does he know you went to see Edgar at Thrushcross Grange?'

'Yes, I told him.'

'Oh dear, Cathy, no wonder he's acting erratically. How did he take that?' Nelly stopped eating, her fork suspended in mid-air thinking about the consequences of my actions. 'You know since he was a boy, Heath has only ever truly loved you.'

Anger boiled inside me again. 'Well, he has a funny way of showing it.'

I calmed down, had a sip of water and returned my focus to the lasagne, even though I had lost my appetite. Eventually, I looked up at Nelly.

'I love Heath, Nelly, I really do.'

'I know you do, Cathy, I've never doubted that,' Nelly said.

'Our souls are made of the same thing, but Edgar's soul is as different as—' I struggled for a comparison.

'A moonbeam from lightning?' Nelly suggested.

'Yes, exactly, thank you, Nelly, I knew you would get it.' I placed my hand over hers. 'I'm so glad you are here with me.'

'I'll always be here for you darling, Cathy,' she said and reached for her handkerchief to dab her eyes.

And then Heath thumped on the door and entered before we could even say 'enter'.

*****

Heath

Everything was going to come to a head this week. Cathy, the business, I just felt it in my bones. I had to go see her.

I stayed away last night because I was so angry I couldn't speak, but I've had all day to brood about it while trying to learn about the new business at the same time. She was doing my head in.

I entered after knocking because Wuthering Heights is technically my family home too and I felt stupid waiting for them to open the door, but I didn't feel right just barging in either. Something about the house never felt like home to me; Hindley had a lot to do with that. Cathy and Nelly turned sharply towards the door, their faces alarmed and then they relaxed seeing it was me. Well, I'm not sure Cathy relaxed, but she didn't look freaked out. I'm sure they'd be talking about me, they looked like I'd caught them in the act.

Nelly jumped up straight away and came over to welcome me; I hugged her and declined the offer of food. I couldn't eat until I'd spoken with Cathy, even though I was starving.

'I was hoping, Cathy, you might come for a walk with me?' I asked, 'after you finish dinner of course.'

Cathy rose. 'I'm finished. We'll just clean up.'

Nelly bustled her away from the table. 'I'll do these, Cathy, I've got all night. Don't walk too far away, Heath, there's a murderer out there.'

'A vigilante,' Cathy said, 'and since we've been reasonably good citizens, we should be right.' She looked at me. 'Well, me anyway,' she said, and smirked.

'I'll look after her, Nelly, don't worry,' I said.

'Can't you just go talk in one of the rooms? I can make myself scarce,' Nelly said.

'I love a night walk,' Cathy said. 'We used to walk at night with Dad all the time years ago.'

The wild child tomboy hadn't left her spirit yet. How will you be with that Edgar, I wondered?

'That was a different time, Cathy. Just be careful,' Nelly said, watching Cathy anxiously.

Cathy grabbed her jacket and with a quick kiss on Nelly's cheek, walked towards the door. I gave Nelly a wave and followed Cathy out into the dark. She took off at a breakneck walking speed and I caught up beside and grabbed her hand, she pulled away. Fine then, let's keep playing this game. I could feel the ice waves coming off her, and from memory, it should be me pissed off given I haven't been kissing other people.

I let her lead the pace for a while and then I'd had a gutful. We reached some huge rocks that we had hid behind many times when we were kids and it provided a great windbreak.

I reached out and grabbed her hand again. 'Just stop, Cathy, just fucking stop!'

She wheeled around on me, pulling her hand out of my grip, her face flushed and beautiful in the chilly night air, and we stood staring at each other. We were both so angry at each other that we'd probably implode before we got a word out.

I turned away from her and looked out across the moors. They were cold, dark and hostile, just like us. I had practised what I was going to say a few hundred times but faced with a wall of cold, I'm not sure it cut it anymore. Can't she tell how different I am? I feel like my life at Wuthering Heights was a hundred years ago. I cut to the chase, 'Are we over, Cathy? Just tell me yes or no and I'll get out of your life.'

Well that didn't work, she snapped to look at me.

'You could have asked that at home and saved us both the trip,' she said.

I scoffed. 'You know, Cathy, I am such an idiot. I had this track playing in my head of how I'd return to you.' I laughed now at the thought. 'You would look at me like I was a new man – connected with family roots, wealthy, well dressed and the owner of a business… successful, ready for our life together. But I never in my wildest dreams thought for a moment you would prefer vanilla, you of all people,' I said, knowing my voice was rising with anger. I tried to check it and continued, '… and that you would give your first kiss to another man.'

Her eyes widened with surprise. She didn't know I had seen her kissing Edgar. I caught her off guard and she looked down and away planning an answer.

The wind was howling around us but we stood in the middle, creating our own storm.

For fuck's sake say something, anything.

'What do you want, Cathy? Just put me out of misery and tell me and if it is not me, then I'll deal with it.' *I'd kill Edgar*, I didn't say that out loud but I was thinking it. 'Tell me it's over, you hate me, you love me, you don't want me… just call it. But…' I warned her, 'I won't ever lose you from my heart, ever. I am completely yours.'

*****

Catherine

I want him so badly I can taste it, but I'm so hurt and so angry and I haven't worked through that yet, and that's partly because he hasn't said what I need to hear. All I've heard is his plans and why he went, but he's back now and I need him to… I don't know… I just need to be us again and that's gone. I need to know he wants me because I'm different now, too. I don't have my parents anymore and I don't have him – I'm older, harder, broken and I don't want to just be the comfort blanket he comes back to, I want to be his everything in the world. Everything is different. He thinks he can wipe a year of pain away with a new suit and a good job!

It is just us, the moors, the wind, and our hearts beating fast. He lets out a ragged breath and I ache for making him so anxious – that same ache I've been feeling for the past year. Yep, I'm hung up on it. I love that he played out our reunion in his head, my hero coming home.

But I don't know how to go forward with him and Edgar is so different. I want to explore that too but the two of them will kill me.

He moves closer to me and I'm frozen on the spot; I'm looking out at the moors trying to answer the kiss accusation. Was it a lucky guess or did he really see me? And then he puts his hands around my waist and pulls me to him. I place my hands on his chest and I can feel his heart pounding, I can feel the heat radiating off him.

It's the strangest feeling. I know these moors intimately;

I know Heath as well as I know myself and yet I feel like I am standing with a stranger in a foreign environment like I'm seeing everything for the first time with different eyes.

'Cathy,' he whispers my name and I look up and make eye contact with him. Big mistake – his eyes are dark and intense, and he is here, the Heath I've always known. I try to pull away but he doesn't release me. I try to find my voice, but I'm torn, frozen.

And then his lips touch mine. I have dreamt of this time. All the times we've held hands, lay in each other's arms, waiting to come of age to make official what we've always known and planned.

I feel him pressing against me, his touch is electric and powerful. His kiss becomes more passionate and deeper as I had always dreamed it would – my fantasy that I played out in my head every time he held my hand or looked at me that way that he does. He was always in my mind, I have watched and felt his pain and his victories and I've never thought we wouldn't be together. But this kiss doesn't compare to my dream, it's like nothing else, it's better – gentle, and yet raw and hungry.

I am completely lost to him.

Chapter 21 - Camp Discover

Catherine

We were on our way to Camp Discover where we went every school year for a week to discover ourselves or something else. I discovered you shouldn't eat the porridge last time, but that's another story. The bus pulled away from the school and we waved obligingly to a couple of parents who stayed to see us off and the teachers we were leaving behind for the week.

'I never thought I'd be excited about going on a school camp,' Tilly said, as she jiggled beside me in the seat.

'And you are?' Jace twisted around from the bus seat in front to face her.

'It's our last one ever,' she said sentimentally, and looked to me for agreement.

I obliged. 'It is, so sad.' I looped my arm through hers. 'No more hikes at sunrise, no more terrible food and team activities—'

'Waiting for a shower until there's no hot water left,' Jace cut in, 'sleeping in bunk beds in a huge room with a whole stack of guys who you wouldn't save if they were drowning – oww!' he exclaimed as Sam, sitting next to him, punched him in the arm.

'Fine then, I'll save you,' Jace said, and got a laugh.

'At least we get out of class and get to wear daggy gear for a week,' Sam said with a shrug.

Jace looked him up and down. 'Mate, how is what you are wearing today any different from other days?'

Tilly and Cathy laughed.

Sam looked down at his gear. 'You can't tell the difference?' he frowned.

Jace rolled his eyes. The boys started talking amongst themselves and I had Tilly to myself.

'Are you okay? You seem sort of distracted,' she asked me.

It was an hour-long bus trip so I told her everything. Tilly's great, her reactions are like she's watching a soap opera, which I guess my life was at the moment.

I finished. 'So, I am seriously looking forward to having a week away from Heath and Edgar so I can try to clear my head.'

Tilly exhaled. 'Cathy, how awful, torn between two lovers.'

'At least it's not torn between two brothers,' I said, and got a laugh before Tilly looked at me. 'Why, do you know two brothers that you like?'

'No.' I gave her a strange look and then nodded to the seat in front of us and Jace. I knew he had caught up with Isabella but I still didn't know if he had told Tilly.

'Any joy?' I asked, lowering my voice.

She looked at the back of Jace's head and shook her own.

'That's going nowhere fast. But I have been messaging Sean, you know, from Daniel's party.'

Great, that was my plan and Sean was nice, not a vampire, which was a good fit for Tilly.

'I really like Sean,' I said and smiled, thinking about him.

'Me too,' she giggled.

One of our sports teachers interrupted our thoughts as he stood up at the front of the bus to make some announcements. And again, my thoughts drifted to Heath and Edgar, Edgar and Heath, anguish.

*****

Hindley

I know I said I'd stop at one, but once Daniel went through the Conversion, we got talking. He said he'd love to just experience the raw power of our nature – like the days when our ancestors used to hunt and kill to live. Then, it was the survival of the species, the weaker didn't stand a chance unless they were protected. Now, we're drinking the best of it bottled for us. Not that we don't appreciate that, Dan and I have had a few good nights in the cellar and then out later for a bit of fun and a girl. But I told him what I'd done.

'You're fucking kidding me,' he said. 'You're the vigilante?'

I smiled and gave him a small nod. 'I was going to stop at one, you know, just to feel what it was like, but then this second opportunity just presented itself,' I said and laughed at my good fortune.

'How?' Daniel asked.

I indicated for him to follow me and we went outside. Daniel's working at the winery doing some graphic design stuff for us during the college holidays. Easy work for him and we pay good rates, especially when it's a mate of mine.

We sat down on a stone fence overlooking one part of the winery and watching as the lunch-a-lot guests and tourists sipped wine on the terrace. The café was a good money-spinner for the business.

I looked around to make sure we could talk with no one hearing us, and then I told him about how I'd met the druggie and cleaned him up for good.

'Then,' I continued, 'I met a chick the other night at a club and she told me her neighbour was always being beaten up by her husband. Can't tell you how we got on the subject but I found out where this woman lived and I cased the husband.'

'Like a hunt,' Daniel said, salivating.

'Love the hunt.'

'And you definitely got the right guy?'

'Oh yeah, I saw his black and blue wife. A tiny thing, and he's this huge fucking wall of a guy,' I said.

'What happened?'

'I followed him for a few nights on his way to the pub after he'd finished dinner and later when he came home that night. He liked his women little, he hit onto a few women at the pub and went home with one of them.'

'Is that the night you got him?' Daniel asked.

'No, I wanted to get him earlier in the night before he

drank too much, so he'd taste better. So the next night I waited and I heard him throwing stuff around inside and I heard her scream. Then he strides out on his way to the pub and I follow him.'

I could feel my eyes flaring with the memory of it. I took a deep breath to stop my teeth from sinking down. I could feel Daniel's blood pumping next to me, he was tasting this story as it went along.

'Go on,' Daniel egged me on.

'Right, so this guy stops when he realises I'm following him and asks me what's my problem. I tell him I knew what he did to his wife and why didn't he try it on someone his own size. So he looks me up and down and laughs because honestly, he was twice me, but he's keen to knock me out so he agrees.'

'What, there?'

'No, he said he knew a place, so I've followed him to the back streets and he doesn't give me any notice, just swings around and takes a hit.'

Daniel laughs because he knows what's coming.

'For a big guy, he could run pretty fast,' I said, and we both chuckled.

'But what was it like?'

I shook my head. 'Like nothing you've ever experienced, my man, I tell you I'm loving these superpowers. The adrenalin pumps through you, your heart is beating like a drum, the blood's pumping, fucking fantastic,' I say, exhaling at the happy memory.

'And the taste?'

'Top shelf.'

‘I want to experience it. I need to,’ Daniel said.

I knew that was coming. I studied him and thought if I don’t do it with him, he’ll go off and do it alone and that might be a sticky situation. You’ve got to leave some blood or spread some around so the body’s not dry.

I nod. ‘Leave it with me, I’ve got someone in mind and the people of The Moors won’t miss him.’

Daniel grinned, his eyes lusting for the hunt and feast already.

Chapter 22 – A dream within a dream

Heath

Cathy's gone for a week; she kisses me and sets every fibre of my being on fire so that I can't sleep, eat or breathe without thinking about her, and now she's gone for a week. Yeah, I am getting some of my own treatment back; the separation is torture.

Good old Camp Discover, I loved going there every year. One week out of home with my friends and no Hindley. Days in nature and not sitting behind a desk listening to the teacher drone on and having such full-on days that at night you just hit the bed and were out of it, totally. It reminds me of our childhood when Cathy and I escaped the house and wandered for hours on the moors. We had our hideouts and caves, our favourite brooks, our favourite trees. Cathy could climb better than anyone I know. I lived for those days that we were on our own and in nature, when we were wild.

This is Cathy's last Camp Discover, but I'll take her camping anytime. I can see our future as clear as if it laid out in front of me. We'll run the winery one day soon; I'll put

Hindley out of business and out of our home, Wuthering Heights. We'll open up the estate more so that the outdoors lives with us... bring in the light and the moors. We'll restore the stables and get a dog or two. We'll surround ourselves with nature and then we'll have a family. Nothing like the family I didn't have or the family I grew up with. Love will surround my family and I'll do whatever I can to protect them and hold us together. I can't wait to begin.

*****

Edgar

She's away on that dreadful school camp and I just want to drive in and rescue her. Man, how cool would that be, showing up, opening the car door and in she jumps. We could just get out of there and go somewhere for a week... the city, London, or over to Paris.

That horrendous Camp Discover they forced us to go on every year was the worse; all I discovered was that people who were dicks at school were dicks out of school as well. The life coping skills they wanted to impart on us existed of sunrise bush walks communing with nature – can't see myself needing that too often, and team trust games. For the love of God, what a circus. I wouldn't trust any of them unless my life depended on it, and even then I'd think twice about it.

Charlotte didn't get the concept of back to nature either; she bought so many changes of wardrobe that you'd think she was shooting an in-nature feature for a glossy. But it made her happy I guess, and she looked great while pretty much everyone else was just roughing it.

Wish I could come and get you, Cathy, I'd take you away from all that. I lie awake some nights thinking about our life; it is going to be so great. You'll move in here – we'll own Thrushcross Grange when Mum and Dad move to Europe in a few years. Isabella can always stay, of course, she's got an entire wing she could live in and never see us unless she wants to. Cathy, you could work in the business if you want or just do your own thing here, whatever that is, or keep working in your family business depending on what's left after Hindley finishes with it.

But before Mum and Dad leave the business, I want to take a year off with Cathy and travel; I want to travel a lot. I've always dreamt of going to every city in the world and experiencing it – there's 197, so it could take a lifetime and that's okay. Cathy would love it. All before we go through the Conversion so we can drink and eat our way around.

When we get home, our home, it will be her house to run. We can have a child or two, a daughter just like Cathy would be the most wonderful thing. I can't wait to marry her and begin.

*****

Catherine

The bus pulls up and we're here!

Tilly and I lifted our bags from the bus storage and follow one of our camp leaders who has separated the boys from the girls. I give Jace a good luck smile and he threatens to see us later.

'Maybe if you are lucky,' I tease him, 'Go bond with the guys. Hunt, fish, talk about girls, sport and cars.'

He rolls his eyes. 'It will be better than talking about boys, shopping and clothes.'

I give him a smirk and wave him off. So here we are, 25 girls ready for a week of discovery, bring it on. As always there's bound to be a few obvious discoveries – like where the boys are staying, how we can sneak in and vice versa.

'C'mon,' Tilly grabbed my hand as we were assigned a bunk room, 'we've got to get bunks near each, away from the window so we don't get woken up by the boys crawling in, and not too close to the door.'

I hurried along behind her. She had it all worked out, and clearly since she'd been messaging Sean there was no one she expected a night visit from in our class. She nearly bowled Morgan and Mia out of the way as she threw herself across two bunks next to each other right in the middle of the dorm.

'Perfect,' she smiled.

I laughed. I would miss this, and I couldn't wait to get outside into the nearby forests and freshwater creeks. We had ten minutes to put our gear in place and meet our cabin leader, who would be the boss for the next week.

'I hope we don't get assigned that cranky bag we had last year,' Tilly said, as she pushed her bag under the bed.

'I didn't see her with the others coming in. They might have sent her off to manage a prison,' I suggested, and Tilly laughed.

We followed the other girls outside and met with the full group again. It was kind of sad to think we'd never be together again like this; our last year and while we spent most of high school busting to get out, now that it was getting closer, it was scary and sad. I half-listened to the programme planned for the week ahead – water adventures, walking and climbing activities, and so on, and thought about how much I wanted to get to the lakes and rugged moors.

'Great, that'll be fun, we haven't done that before,' Tilly said, nudging me.

Damn, I missed what she was saying again, sigh.

'Not sure about the gorge walking though.' She frowned.

Good grief, gorge walking! I tuned back in as the camp leader promised a week of mind and body fulfilment – great because I'm going out of my mind. I felt trapped, like I had to make some decision, and fast. I didn't want to hurt Edgar, and I couldn't bear to hurt Heath, but I don't know what I want.

I love Edgar's stillness. He has this quiet, sexy power about him… I saw it when I walked into the dance with him. Every girl wanted to be with him. It's like he radiates power and sophistication.

The problem is that I'm pretty sure Edgar thinks I'm a china doll. He thinks I'm sweet and lovely, ladylike and feminine. And I'm not. I can be, but for how long? What if I swear or want to have everyone over? What if I don't want to work in his business or my family business? What if I can't live up to his image of me?

Heath is the opposite in every respect. With him, it will always be the familiar and he knows me because I am Heath. Our spirits match but will he ground me? Will my life always be Wuthering Heights, the business, and Heath, forever and ever? He may look polished now and successful but I know him, I can see what he is and he is raw at heart, untrusting and wary. Years of pain have made him that way and there's not enough polish in the world to make him anything but that. If I stay with Heath, then I too am that, because I have lived all his humiliations and anger and pain. I am Heathcliff.

I am so torn.

Chapter 23 – Missing

Catherine

I woke to the smell of nothing cooking, so I knew I wasn't at home. Thank God for the bread rolls on camp, you can make a meal of them. I had slept well, probably because we didn't all stop talking until well after midnight, so I was pretty exhausted by the time we slept. It was nice to not spend the night awake and stressing out.

First light and I was a morning person, up and at it. Tilly, buried under her blankets, was not. She wouldn't surface until the get-up gong sounded. I looked around the bunk and saw a few girls were up. I quietly grabbed my gear and headed for the shower. It was a gorgeous day and my first thoughts went to Heath; I knew he'd be awake. Maybe out running. I wonder if he lay away at night thinking of me as I thought of him. I wonder if he randomly slept with other girls now that he was out of Wuthering Heights and had his share place with Aden. I said hello to a few of my classmates that I passed on the way to the shower and entered the cubicle. At least first thing in the morning there was plenty of hot water.

As I showered, my thoughts went to Edgar. I knew he got up in the morning and went swimming. He had that swimming physique –broad shoulders, slim hips. I could imagine him gliding up and down the pool, rhythmically knocking over his required laps. Both of them in their solitary pursuits. Are you thinking of me too, Edgar? I got out, dried off and put on my track wear, ready for this morning's activity whatever that was. Bring it on.

The gong rang out so by the time I got back to our barracks, everyone was dressing and making their beds. Tilly was quiet, she couldn't form many words in the morning, so I suspected she'd catch up by mid-morning. None of us could have imagined that by the end of the day, two of our group would be missing, and all hell would break loose.

*****

Heath

Today I've got a meeting with the Linton representatives about the Blood Bank proposal. They've got a few more questions about distribution and one that I've been suspecting and Edgar hinted they'd be asking – why, given my family background, I didn't put the offer to Hindley and keep the business with the Earnshaws rather than coming to them first. Really, do they need to ask? But it's good they have a few questions, it means they are looking at the proposal seriously.

I know this will probably sound super gross, but I'm being trying to detect Cathy's scent in the air. Camp Discover is only about an hour away by car, so it's not like she's gone to a foreign country, and since I'm getting triggers and developing at a weird pace, I thought I might smell her. There's no rule book for hybrids, whereas there is for the Immortalis. I guess because the hybrids can be a combo of a few different things and in different strengths. Because I haven't had the Conversion yet, I don't know what will be the strongest part of me – werewolf or vampire, but right now, the werewolf is dominating. I wonder when it will peak… when I turn 21 or will it just keep getting stronger?

I feel it changing me, and running wild the other night after my encounter with Cathy was the most amazing feeling – like I was truly alive and every muscle in my body was working to full strength. My sense of smell and hearing are out of this world, and I can see things with such clearness from so far away, it's like a superpower. I'm yet to see what happens when it is a full moon but I read up on what happens at the library – okay, it was on a fanfiction site, but hey there must be some truth in it since all the stories, even the really old ones, have werewolves at full strength in a full moon.

I also have to be careful because I'm hearing conversations around me and I have to remember that they did not include me in them! Could be very handy in love and life. I wish I could read minds, that might come later. I'd love to be in Cathy's head, knowing what she's thinking, what she sees in Edgar.

It's kind of weird that it has only hit me now; it's like the body knows that you have come of age. It's probably a good thing – imagine a kid with these powers. I wish I had an ancestor I could talk to from the werewolf side of the family. From what the solicitor said, I'm it. But I can't pick up Cathy's scent yet; I'll keep trying.

*****

Hindley

So the Lintons are ready to talk business, ha, this should be interesting. They've got no choice but to accept my offer. I can't believe Dad let them rip the family off like that for years. Once I get the right profit margin set up, then it's time to think about Wuthering Heights. I don't know if Heath is living there anymore or not, but now with Dad gone, it's time he moved back to the gutter where he came from. And if Nelly and Cathy don't like it, they can pack up and move as well.

That house will be mine and whoever the lucky lady is that I settled down with, I thought, amusing myself. I don't need any hangers-on. It's going to be a big week. Tonight, Daniel and I are going hunting; Heath doesn't know it yet, but it's his last week of life. I don't think he needs to be the work of the vigilante – that might cast some suspicion on what he did wrong and whether he's worthy of death. Given everyone knows we hate each other, the spotlight might turn on me. No, I think once Daniel and I have had our fun hunting him and feasted, we'll just bury him deep where he won't be discovered.

As far as anyone knows, he's run off again; the only one who will care will be Cathy, and maybe because he's done it again, she'll be over him and wash her hands of him. Then she can focus on Edgar so we can get them partnered and I can start working at owning that side of the family too. God, I love being in business. If Dad took a lesson of ruthlessness from me instead of always preaching about fair business, we'd have owned half the village years ago. I was so ambitious I could taste it, and I'll enjoy tasting the Hybrid's blood along with it.

*****

Catherine

There were three things we all agreed on and three things we weren't sure about. We sat around the campsite, tired and wired. The 10-kilometre hike was beautiful, but hilly and required a lot of concentration. Back from it, we were on edge as the police and rescue services interviewed us and our stressed-out camp supervisors.

We agreed there were twelve of us when we started the trek and now there were ten. We agreed that best friends Leila and Stephanie were definitely on the trek when it started, and they were still with us when we reached the summit and stopped for lunch. We agreed that no one saw anyone else except our group and team leaders during the entire length of the trek. No strangers, no vigilante turned cold-blooded murderer.

After that, things got sketchy. No one could remember if they came down with us from the summit, or seeing them when we stopped for a swim at the lake. Tilly and I were sure, well, pretty sure, we saw Leila and Stephanie ahead of us on the walk down, but Nat, Chloe and Carla, who were in front of us, couldn't remember seeing them at all.

No one could agree on what they were wearing to help with descriptions of clothing for the rescue service and police, and since taking our phones with us was banned, no one had any shots or selfies with them. See phones are good!

And we couldn't agree if there were other paths that they could have accidentally veered off on or if we heard their voices yelling out because we were a fairly noisy group. One of our group thought she heard a scream, but it could have been a bird. We were hopeless really; we wouldn't have been recruited for spies.

It was totally weird – how do you just disappear out of sight? Well, actually it's probably not that hard given the number of trees, rocks and paths here, but it's not like we're the quietest group. If you were lost, couldn't you hear twelve girls going up and coming down the mountain and try to catch up with us?

There was another thing too, which only I and one other girl in my class knew, Stephanie is one of us – her parents are Immortalis and she wasn't planning on her Conversion for years yet. She had no sensory skills to help her, and if the unthinkable happens, like if she is dead out there, then she'll be lost to us forever like Saps are. Freaky stuff.

Tilly grabbed my hand and lowered her voice as she said what everyone was thinking.

'What if the vigilante is not good after all and he or her has attacked them?'

I squeezed her hand and nodded. 'It went through my mind too.'

Thank God it wasn't Heath. I believed him when he said he wasn't the killer, but if he knows who is, are they capable of this?

Everyone around us looked pale and worried, except for maybe one or two who were kind of enjoying the drama, and making sure they looked okay if media converged on the site. Sigh. Our camp instructor then called for attention and gave us all a list of instructions, including no talking to the media, and we had thirty minutes to pack as the bus would come in an hour to take us home – a one day camp! We were all getting our phones back as well to contact family and let them know we are okay, since they had contacted Leila and Stephanie's parents now.

There was such a weird buzz in the air – tension, fear, excitement, mystery – and by the time we had finished packing, lots and lots of villagers and the media had arrived wanting to help with the search and find out what was going on. A lot of the parents raced here. I wish mine were still around to do so – it was a stab in the heart to be reminded that no one was racing to pick me up. The rescue service began dividing people into teams. Tilly's mum arrived and getting out of the car she ran towards us as though she couldn't believe it was Tilly who hadn't disappeared.

It relieved Tilly to see her; I think she was internally freaking out. Her mum wanted to give me a lift home too, but I saw Hindley pulling up in the car park, Daniel with him, so I thanked her, and gave Tilly a quick hug and went to meet them.

They greeted Tilly and her mum as they passed; Luckily, Tilly recovered enough to give Hindley her best smile. The boys came over to me.

'Hey guys, are you here to help search?' I asked.

Hindley put his arm around my shoulder in a rare show of affection and we headed towards the search group.

'Hindley thought we might help with our extra skills,' Daniel said discreetly.

'Know anything more?' Hindley asked me.

'Nothing,' I said. 'They just didn't come back with us and we all remember seeing them at lunch and then they just… vanished. You don't think it's the vigilante, do you? People are suggesting it.'

Hindley laughed, and then looked at me with a direct, intense look. 'I assure you, it wasn't him.'

I was about to question him when I heard my name called. I turned around and Heath was getting out of his car in the car park.

I swear Hindley made this growling sound. 'I'll see you later,' he said, and nudging Daniel, they headed to the search group.

I ran over to Heath and he wrapped me in his arms.

'Thank God you're okay, I just heard.' He held me for a moment, and I felt so safe against his chest, absorbing his strength. Then he held me at arm's length. 'I can take you straight home if you like, then I'll come back and join the search party.'

I shook my head. 'It's okay. I'll go on the bus with the others that are still here. I'm glad you're going to help.'

'What's Hindley doing here?' he asked.

‘Same as you,’ I said, turning and watching Hindley and Daniel as they joined a search team. ‘They can use their new senses,’ I reminded him.

‘Okay, promise me you’ll just get on the bus and go straight home until they’re found,’ he said, pushing a strand of hair back behind my ear. ‘Promise me, Cathy?’

‘Yes, Dad,’ I teased, and he grinned.

He was adorable when he was protective. It made me realise I hadn’t heard from Edgar. Perhaps he didn’t know about the missing girls yet.

‘I promise. But I’m not in any danger… and Steph and Leila probably just took a wrong turn and everything will turn out fine.’

‘I hope so,’ he said with a look to the top of the summit.

‘Who’s the vigilante, Heath?’ I asked.

He snapped to look at me, surprised by the question.

‘I can’t say, it’s not for me to say… don’t ask me.’ He looked away.

‘Okay. Then I know it is someone you know or someone close to you.’

He didn’t answer. I let it drop. ‘Call me when you finish?’ I asked him.

‘Sure.’

‘Be careful. It’s going to be dark in about three hours and cold.’ I shuddered and looked towards the summit. I hope they found Steph and Leila before nightfall. We were all just wearing long-sleeve Ts and jeans, nothing that would keep you warm out there.

‘It’ll be fine, just go,’ he said.

He gave me a discreet and quick kiss and turned me toward my friends.

'Get going you,' he said, bossing me.

I smiled at him and left to join the girls. The bus was just turning into the car park and couldn't get a park so just parked everyone in. No one was leaving before us, anyway. I turned back and Heath was watching me walk toward the bus. I hope he'd be okay – I didn't like Hindley and Heath to be anywhere near each other if I could avoid it. Then my phone rang – Edgar at last. It was nice to feel loved, even without Mum and Dad at home waiting for my return. I answered as I grabbed my bag and followed the other girls onto the bus. A television crew was filming us so we kept our heads down, except for Jacinta and Lilly, who I swear flicked their hair back, stuck their chests out and walked as slowly as they could towards the bus. Good grief, did they think this was going to launch their modelling careers?

'Hi Edgar,' I said, as I got on board.

'You're okay?' he said, and exhaled.

'I'm fine, but thank you for calling.' I sat down next to Natalie, who was also on the phone.

'I'll come and get you,' Edgar said.

'It's okay, I'm with my friends and we're getting the bus back, I've just boarded.' I looked out the window to see Heath disappearing into the woods with a team. Then I saw Hindley and Daniel leave the group they were in and follow Heath.

I told Edgar I'd call him back, let the camp instructor know my brother was giving me a lift, and got off the bus. This was not good, not good at all.

Chapter 24 – The reckoning

Catherine

Arrivals packed the car park like a scene at a major concert. I moved towards the continually growing numbers of searchers; a stack of groups including Heath, Hindley and Daniel had just disappeared along the bush tracks and now more volunteer searchers were arriving by the minute. I dumped my bag down beside the other packs and before anyone noticed me and sent me back to the bus, I grabbed one of the yellow vests, put it on, and blended in with the group. I had to catch up with Heath's group and warn him. Or at least catch up with Hindley and ask him what the hell he was playing at. I couldn't move straight to the path and follow them on my own, I had to join a group or I'd get a bollocking for creating another missing person opportunity, so I waited impatiently.

I listened in to the instructions, nodding away like everyone else and trying not to draw attention to myself. If they didn't hurry and catch up with the other groups, Hindley and Heath would kill each other before I could get there. Behind me, I heard noises and turned to see a man and woman arriving. I'm guessing they are Leila's parents, as I know Stephanie's parents from our Immortalis gatherings. They were stressed out, as you'd expect, and Stephanie's mum was crying.

Finally, the large party broke into five groups and I buried myself at the back of the one going in the same direction as the two men from my life, Heath and Hindley. Everyone was fired up so no one noticed, and there were other women in my group that had come to search, including a young woman who was saying how she regularly walked in this area and knew the paths well. *Whatever, let's go here!*

We started at last and I took up the rear; I kept my eyes and ears peeled, trying to spot the boys. I wish I had some sensory power so I could smell them or see them from afar. One benefit of the Conversion.

We must have been walking for about fifteen minutes when we saw another group off on our left; I scanned the faces and back of heads, but the boys weren't in that group. I kept forgetting to look for the girls while I looked out for Heath and Hindley – why didn't they both just stay away! Then five minutes later, I spotted Daniel. *At last!* But where were the other two? I dropped slightly behind the searchers in front of me, and when the group had turned on the trail, I darted over to him. It surprised him to see me.

'Hey weren't you on the bus?' he asked.

'I was, but then I saw Hindley following Heath and I had to get off and do something. This is not good Daniel.'

He nodded. 'I know.' He ran his hand through his hair and looked back to where he had just come from.

'Why aren't you with them?' I asked.

'We had a fight about a few things including following Heath, so Hindley told me to get lost,' Daniel said, 'I was just debating what to do… go back, let them kill each other, or get someone who knows the two of them to intervene – and I don't think that should be you!' he said, warily.

Great.

'It's me,' I told him. 'Where are they? I have to find them.' I glanced in the direction he was looking towards. 'That way?'

'Cathy, don't.' He grabbed my arm. He was stronger now that he had undergone his Conversion. His eyes drew me in – beautiful, sharp and hypnotising. I looked away quickly in case he tranced me out of it.

'It's dangerous,' he continued.

I shook my arm free of him. 'I know, Daniel, I've lived with it all my life.'

'What does Hindley want? Why did he follow him? He's so obsessive in his hate sometimes,' he said.

Daniel turned as a twig snapped behind us, but it was just another search group taking the trail beside us.

'You two alright?' a guy in a team leader's orange vest yelled out.

'All good thanks, mate,' Daniel waved back, and I gave him a smile to show there was nothing to see here, move along.

'Daniel?' I pushed him. 'What else did you and Heath fight about?'

He dug his hands into his jean pockets and breathed out as he worked out what to tell me.

'We haven't time, please, just tell me.' I tugged at his arm.

Daniel took my hand and pulled me further into the bush away from the main trail. 'I didn't tell you this, okay?'

'Okay, what?' I pushed him.

He lowered his voice. 'Hindley is the vigilante.'

'No!' I didn't want to believe it. My mind was racing. I just knew it would be one of the new Conversions… or Heath, but he promised me it wasn't him. I felt guilty now for secretly doubting him. But why wouldn't he tell me it was Hindley? He's got no loyalty to him… ah, I bet he was protecting me from being hurt or worried.

Daniel continued. 'Hindley said the first two victims were justified and the community was thanking him. He said he had a third person in mind that we could share… you know, try my first real hunt. Then it turns out to be your step-brother.'

'Oh my God! He's done nothing wrong, honestly, Daniel, he's a good person.'

'I know,' he assured me, 'that's why I said no, and Hindley told me to shove off basically and took off.'

'Which way, I've got to stop him. Heath will retaliate… he's had a lifetime of putting up with that crap and he won't take it any longer.' I started heading into the bush. 'This way?'

He nodded and caught up with me. 'I'm coming with you,' he said.

'You don't have to,' I assured him as I ducked and weaved between low branches and twigs that earlier walkers hadn't snapped.

‘Don’t be crazy,’ he said. ‘I’m not letting you face them alone. Let’s go.’

He moved past me and took the lead, he was going much faster with his new skills, faster than I could keep up with. He had to keep stopping to wait for me, remembering he was an Immortalis now.

‘I could carry you,’ he said, and I nodded.

I climbed onto his back and we went at breakneck speed. In a matter of minutes, we heard them before we saw them.

The most terrifying sounds I’ve ever seen, and then they came into sight.

*****

Heath

This guy knows no boundaries. For the love of God, I’m here to help rescue two girls that I remember well from the year below at school, to subtly lend my werewolf sensory skills to the search and he’s following me. I let the group get ahead and turn to face him.

‘Really Hindley, here and now?’

‘He’s right mate, let’s go,’ his friend Daniel said, grabbing Hindley’s arm. Daniel was an alright guy, don’t know why he hung around with Hindley.

Hindley brushed him off.

‘This is our next bad citizen,’ Hindley said with a grin. ‘The vigilantes are here for you Heath, time for restitution.’

‘Yeah?’ I asked. ‘Just wondering what my crime might be?’

We stood staring at each other like two bullies in the playground. Both with our own strengths, his a little more developed than mine since I was a fledgling Werewolf and I hadn't undertaken the Vampire Conversion yet. Daniel stepped back. He was strong enough to take us both now, but he always had a moral compass, he used to come to the house with his parents when we were kids and if Hindley wasn't around, he'd join Cathy and me for adventures on the moors.

'Your crimes?' Hindley said, rocking on his heels and looking satisfied with himself. 'So many. How about the way you stealthily came into my home and won my father over with your deception and games – he favoured you over me in the end, over his son? Do you know what he told me a few months before he died? That he wanted me to be more like you… to spend as much time as you did learning the business, to understand how to be firm but fair, to be kind to people from all walks of life.' Hindley laughed. 'What a crock of shit. He was weak and you're no better.'

This would never end with Hindley, not until one of us was dead, and I'd rather that was him than me. But Cathy would never forgive me if I killed her brother; it was a no-win situation for me. In the background I could hear volunteers shouting out to the girls, hitting items to make noise if the girls could hear them and follow the noise to safety. I was hoping a group of them would wander near us and break this up. It wasn't the time or place. I delivered my best line.

'Yep,' I said, 'not sure how your failings make me a villain, but you were always a self-centred prick, Hindley, just like *your* dad said.'

That enraged him. I saw the veins pulse in his face, his eyes flared and his new sharp teeth bared in his grimace.

'Let's just back off and cool down, hey guys,' Daniel said. 'We've only got a few hours of light left to find the girls and this is not the time for a dual.'

'But this one is all yours, Daniel,' Hindley said, offering me up. He ran his tongue over his teeth in anticipation. 'I'll help you bring him down. Do you want him or not?' Hindley asked with a glance to Daniel.

'You're kidding me, aren't you?' Daniel asked. 'Let's go, Hindley, stop being an idiot.'

Hindley shook his head. 'Whatever. You go, I've got work to do here.'

Daniel glanced at me and I gave him a nod of the head to tell him to go. He headed back on the path. I don't know if he's going to keep people away or get help to break it up, but it sure as hell would not be pretty.

Then, with lightning speed that made a blur of him, Hindley attacked.

*****

Catherine

The noise – the growling terrified me, the sounds of pain. I couldn't get there fast enough and then Daniel stopped near them and I dropped from his back and cried out. They were both covered in blood – on their faces, their shirts. They were both wounded, limping around each other like a macabre dance of the villains.

Hindley's teeth were exposed, his veins pumping and his eyes wild. Heath hadn't fully converted to his hybrid form, I don't know why, but he was definitely part animal and holding his own – he was fierce, larger, extended. Both of their faces were animalistic and ugly in battle.

'Stop, both of you,' I cried and ran into them. Daniel tried to grab me and missed and I know it was a stupid thing to do, but I know neither of them would harm me. I hadn't counted on them not seeing me until too later and being caught in their movements that were too fast to prevent contact. I don't know who I hit or how, but I hit the ground hard and I couldn't move. My shoulder felt like it was out, pain roared up my neck and back and arm, and as I blacked out I saw Heath's stricken face as he bent over me.

Chapter 25 – Lives forever altered

Catherine

When I opened my eyes I was in a sterile-like room, wearing a hospital gown with some beautiful flowers on the bed table beside me. Heath sat in the chair beside me and, on seeing me awake, rose to get the nurse. I stopped him.

'Hindley?' I asked after my brother.

'Still alive,' he answered, and left the room to call the nurse. I winced and looked down. I had some traction on my arm, but otherwise, everything I moved seemed to respond okay. Breathing was a little hard and I had a dull ache around my ribs.

He came back with the nurse; his face was full of concern. I know he didn't start it, but I don't want to see him or Hindley. I just want to know if Steph and Leila were found and then be alone for a bit. It'd be good if Tilly came by.

'Welcome back, Catherine,' the nurse said. She was about Mum's age and her face was kind. The name on her badge was Rosemary. 'How are you feeling?'

'I'm not sure yet,' I said truthfully. 'Have I been out long?'

'Just a few hours. You have a concussion, a few sprains, a dislocation and a broken rib.'

'Really?' I said, shocked and glanced at Heath.

'We'd like just to keep you in overnight, but you can head home tomorrow. The doctor will catch you on his rounds later tonight.'

'Thank you,' I said, and she smiled and left.

'Cathy, I'm—'

I cut him off. 'Did they find Steph and Leila?'

He sat down on the high stool next to my bed. 'Yes, they're alive, but it's not all good news.'

I groaned. 'Tell me.'

Heath continued. 'Lord knows how, but it appears they stopped to take a selfie, got separated from the rest of your group, and then wandered around until they got too close to a ledge and it collapsed on them. They fell down an enormous drop. Leila is not so bad, she was behind Stephanie and broke a few bones, but Stephanie is really bad.'

I tried to read his face. 'How bad?'

'That bad,' he said, knowing what I was thinking.

'No!'

'She fell about 10 metres and hit a rock. Her skull… you don't need to know, but she was barely alive when they found her. Her Dad got her, could sense her.'

'Of course,' I said. 'So what happens now?' I glanced at the doorway to make sure no one could hear her.

'Steph and Leila were both in here, but Steph's parents have said they are taking her home and getting a specialist in. They've gone straight to the Dome and an elder is undertaking the Conversion.'

'Oh, wow. I know Steph wasn't going to convert until she was thirty, this will devastate her. She wanted a family and all that stuff.'

'But she'll be alive, so that's the main thing. Not such a bad thing to always be young and beautiful, and better than being dead,' Heath said with a shrug.

'Hmm, well I know Daniel had a crush on her so now they're going to be around the same age forever. But she'll have to go away or go undercover for a few months – enough time to let people think she healed naturally,' I said.

'I'm sure they'll do the usual, you know, go overseas for special therapy or some crap,' Heath mumbled, disinterest in his voice as he wanted to get to the main topic.

With that out of the way, I turned my attention to him.

'Beautiful flowers, my favourite,' I said.

'I know. Cathy, I didn't provoke that. I'm so sorry you had to see it and then get caught in it. What the hell were you thinking?'

'I was thinking you two are idiots and if I didn't get there, you'd kill each other. What happened after you both wiped me out?'

'Daniel and Hindley got you to help. They could do it speedily without…'

'Shape changing?' I asked.

'Something like that.' Heath looked out the window beside my bed and I knew he was keeping something from me, I could read all his body language and expressions.

Sometimes I think we know each other better than we know ourselves.

'Where's it going to go, Heath? This whole feud with you and Hindley? It has to end, so how's it going to play out?' I asked and pushed myself up in a more comfortable position. He reached for the water, gave it to me and returned it to the bench top when I finished.

'When one of us dies,' he said.

'No, don't say that. There has to be a way to call a true,' I said, my heart lurching.

Heath shook his head. 'There'll be no truce.'

I exhaled with impatience. 'There's something else, isn't there? Something you're not telling me?' I asked.

He returned his attention to me.

'Yes. I'm sorry Cathy but Hindley's been arrested.'

'Holy crap! Why?' I sat up and yelped with pain before dropping back again.

'They have charged him with the two murders, the vigilante murders,' Heath said. 'And no, before you ask, I never told. I've always known, so why would I bother telling now?'

'Was it Daniel? Did he reveal it?'

'No. I suspect it was DNA,' Heath said.

'How? Hindley doesn't have any DNA on record.'

Heath stood and walked around the room. 'The bloodied clothes that were left on the mountain after our fight – Hindley left his shirt. It was found and the police took it with them. Maybe they thought it was connected to the girls because they hadn't found them at that stage, or maybe they thought it had something to do with the past murders. I guess they prioritised the DNA testing given the number of murders in town.'

'But how would they know it's Hindley's shirt?'

'It was his football shirt, it's labelled,' Heath said.

I felt sick. What now? How do we get Hindley off? Can he claim self-defence, they were both crims after all? Or maybe he could just escape with his Conversion powers and leave the village, but then he'd leave everything that is his, plus his family and friends.

'You know what this means?' Heath asked.

I turned my attention back to him. I didn't know what it would mean for Hindley. A good solicitor, the best we could get, will know Hindley's chances, but then I realised that's not what Heath meant.

'What? What does it mean?'

'With Hindley out of the way, I'm in charge of the business, and when you graduate from school, you will be in charge with me. We can run the winery together, Cathy, how Dad wanted it to be run.'

'What? I can't really think about that now. I've got to get help for Hindley,' I said, my mind racing. 'Besides, you've just bought a business...'

'The winery is my family birthright too,' he said. 'Our father wanted it that way, and I will uphold all his good work, including the current business arrangement with the Linton family. Besides, there are good people already working in my Blood Bank business who can step up and manage that for me.'

'Whatever,' I said angrily. I couldn't concentrate on that; I couldn't believe we were even talking business with Hindley locked up in jail, charged with murder. My head was spinning, and then the worse thing occurred to me.

'Heath!' I exclaimed. 'Hindley won't survive in there without blood. He'll get weaker and weaker. We need to get blood to him.'

Heath shook his head. His eyes narrowed. 'Cathy, it's too much asking me to do that.'

'But for me, he's your stepbrother,' I implored him.

'You're kidding me, aren't you?' Heath hissed. 'I'd walk the globe for you, Cathy, but I will never, ever, help Hindley. Ask Edgar to do it, I'm sure he will.'

As soon as he said the words, Edgar appeared in the hallway. Seeing Heath, he gave a wave and came into my room. The boys greeted each other with cool indifference, and he came over and kissed me on the cheek.

'Are you okay? How horrendous for you,' he said.

I'm pathetic, I don't know why, but I began to tear up. It had just been such a long and dramatic day and now Hindley was in trouble. He was my only living blood relative.

'I'm okay, but I'm terrified for Hindley,' I said, and sniffed in an unladylike manner. I reached for the box of tissues.

'I can't believe he's the one, the vigilante,' Edgar said. 'But on the upside, it's good at least that his crimes were vigilante-based, not cold-blooded murder – the damage to the business won't be too bad.'

I couldn't believe he thought I was worried about the business. What the hell is wrong with Heath and Edgar?

No one seemed to care what happened to my brother while locked up.

Heath cleared his throat. 'I'm sure that's the last thing on Cathy's mind right now,' he said, like some saint.

Edgar took my hand. 'Of course, sorry. Anyway, I've spoken to the Doctor and you can leave in the morning. I've got the guest room and bathroom being prepared. You can stay with Isabella and me until you are back on your feet. I'll get whatever help you need.'

I smiled at him gratefully. I looked into his beautiful, calm face and released a breath. He had taken charge so easily, with no violence, just cool sophistication. And now I was invited to recuperate in his beautiful, light-filled home.

'That's so kind,' I said.

'Not at all,' he said with a slight shrug.

'Will your folks be okay with that?' I asked him.

'They insist on it. So you'll come?' he said.

'Thank you, yes.'

I think I heard Heath grunt some kind of goodbye as he stormed out of the room, and a piece of my broken heart went with him.

*****

Heath

I would do anything for Cathy, anything except what she just asked me to do. She can't seriously think after ten years of abuse by her dead-shit brother I'd be the one taking him blood in jail. I hope he dehydrates, shrivels up and dies. I'd like to be there to watch it happen. The slower the better. Too much? No way. I can still see the cruel sneer on his face each time he beat me and his look of sheer enjoyment. I know I can reciprocate that.

Cathy saw Hindley follow me into the woods, how long does she seriously think I'm going to put up with him pushing me around? Then Edgar rides in on his bloody white horse, all squeaky clean and shiny and has fixed everything. Bravo.

Well, things have changed and if I have anything to do with it, Hindley will never get out of jail and I can't believe my good luck. I never thought it would happen so soon, but now I'm stepping up. I'll be running the winery and blood wine deliveries, and the blood bank. The Lintons don't have to change anything or do additional deals. I'm the man at the top and I say, onward and upward – let's go. I'm moving back to Wuthering Heights and now it will be mine and Cathy's home, Nelly's too.

There's only one fly in the ointment. When is Cathy coming home to me?

*****

Hindley

So thirsty. It's all I can think about… I can hear the blood pumping in the guards' necks as they pass by my cell. I just want to grab one of them and drink him dry. Christ, how long can I go on like this? I'm such an idiot; I can't believe I left my shirt up there, although seriously, who would have thought the cops would associate it with anything going on? Yeah, probably everyone. It's the hybrid's fault. I was so caught up in the moment and destroying him. I've blown everything. Heath will take over the business, manage the house, be exactly what Dad wanted him to be. I'm the born leader, not him. How does he get to rise from the gutter to inherit everything that belongs to me? I've got to get out of here and destroy him.

Where the hell is Cathy and why hasn't she been to see me? How bad are her injuries, a broken arm or something? Whatever! She knows I need blood. Get discharged and get here now!

I hear the keys rattle in the outside gate and turn to watch the hallway, and the guard walks down towards me. You never know which of us caged animals he's going to let out, but this time he comes to me.

'Someone here to see you, Earnshaw,' he says. I have to put my own handcuffs on and then he unlocks the door. Can't believe this shit is happening to me. I follow him down the hallway. He's a bloody disgrace to his uniform, this guy – overweight, scruffy, I could destroy him in a minute and everyone in here, but I'll play the game. Please God, let it be Cathy waiting to see me. I can see the meeting room now and it's not her. Damn, it's the solicitor. I won't be able to talk with him when all I can focus on is his blood pumping around his body. I have to drink.

'Hindley,' he says and rises as I sit opposite him. He asks the guard to uncuff me and surprisingly the guard agrees but locks us both in the meeting area.

My solicitor, Maurice Blackhearth, looks like he's spent the morning getting ready. His suit is top class, he's probably in his sixties but he's trim, tall, sophisticated. His hair is grey and he has just enough facial hair to be cool. He has been my family's lawyer for three decades. He's a Sap; his folks were Immortalis and he chose not to do the Conversion. I don't get that. Why would you want to live a normal life, at risk of dying any day, aging every minute, subject to pain and illness? Nope, totally lost on me. Although I remember some story about him being in love. Whatever, I want his blood.

He exhales likes he's going to give me bad news and then he does.

'I'll lay it on the line for you Hindley, it will not be easy to get you off,' he says.

I can barely hear what he's saying to me because my thirst is overpowering me and I can hear his heartbeat like it is my own.

'If you'd just knocked off the druggie, then I'd have a good chance of getting you off – most of the village supports what you did. But the other body...'

'I need blood, Maurice, urgently,' I say in a low, menacing voice. I watch his body stiffen, his eyes quickly go to the door, but we're alone. I know he's trying to steady his heart rate. I can hear it and smell his rise in adrenalin. He continues as though he didn't hear me. Odd tactic... stalling.

'Unfortunately, the domestic violence kill, well the wife loved him allegedly, he's got two young kids and his parents are stupid enough to think he was a fine, upstanding citizen. They want justice,' he concludes.

I nod. 'I know it's not going to be easy Maurice, thanks for taking me on.' I throw him a bone. 'But I have to drink. I need to get regular blood or regular donor visitors and I desperately need it now.'

He nods and stupidly moves his head slightly, which only draws my attention to his neck. I am so thirsty.

He swallows and extends his arm across the table. 'If you are quick and can dull the pain—'

He doesn't have to finish the sentence before I lower my head to his wrist. He braces in fright and closes his eyes, and I've stopped before he realises it. I glance into his eyes, tell him he doesn't remember me drinking, and run my finger over the marks on his wrist to reduce them. I could have had so much more, but I didn't want him to be too weak to walk out.

That will only temporarily sate me. I keep thinking of the entire cellar of top-shelf blood wine at the winery and my head spins. I'm going to die here.

Chapter 26 - Call to action

Catherine

It's been eight days since the hospital staff discharged me and I am desperate to see Hindley and Heath. It's all I've thought about for days… Hindley, Heath, Hindley, Heath – it's the story of my life. I can't eat, I can't sleep and I can't get any answers. I'm scared Hindley will die in jail, and I don't know who is supplying blood to him. The irony is not lost on me; my school friend Stephanie has to undergo the Conversion to survive after her fall, and if only Hindley hadn't gone through the Conversion yet, none of this would have happened – no vigilante, and well, maybe he might not have taken on Heath, he probably would have waited until he had the power to do so.

My body is black and blue – seriously, I've never seen such dark bruising. Running into a hybrid werewolf-not yet vampire and a new fledgling vampire wasn't one of my best ideas; it was like hitting two speeding trains and being thrown sky-high. Edgar insists I stay housebound for a while longer while I recover, and Nelly – who has moved here to look after me and Edgar and Isabella while their folks are away for a brief time – agrees with him. But she keeps bemoaning the fact I look so awful because I'm not sleeping or eating. I feel so isolated; I've tried to head out a dozen times, but they have ushered me back to bed, it's like they are all on a Cathy roster system!

I can't wait to go back to school next week when school holidays are over so I can have a life again. Seriously, who has ever said that in their life? Clearly, I'm not well. I want to go home to Wuthering Heights too, I wish Mum and Dad were here, everything would be different. I'm going crazy – Isabella is so sweet I could kill her and Edgar is so kind with his love and attention, I'm drowning in it. I'm stifled. I need to be out on the moors again; I need to breathe the fresh air and surrounded myself with nothing but nature – no walls.

The other thing that is driving me to the edge is the quiet. The Linton mansion is on the other side of the hill from Wuthering Heights, so Thrushcross Grange is wind protected. It is abnormally quiet – I can't hear the moors at all or the wind rushing across it. At Wuthering Heights, it's all I've ever known. The wind there wakes me at night, rattles my windows; sometimes I'd wake when it didn't rattle them because it was too quiet. When I'm out on the moors, the wind will push me along in the direction it was heading, whisper and roar in my ears so I can think of nothing but that moment in time. But here, it is as silent as a tomb, except for the constant flow of people around me.

I need to be away from here, I need Heath. Where is he?

Why hasn't he come to me? I grab my phone and check when I last called and messaged him. Yeah, too soon to do so again. I've checked out all his friends' online accounts and he's not featuring in any photos or mentions. What is he doing? I know he is angry at me for going home with Edgar. I know it wasn't his fault with Hindley, but if he loves me, he could take blood to Hindley, for me. Why doesn't he come? Is he out on the moors without me? Is he living at home at Wuthering Heights without me and running our business and going to work every day and not thinking of me?

I get off the bed and feel the pain shooting up my back and neck. I wait a moment until the pain and dizziness subside and my eyes can refocus on what is around me. I pace slowly around the room; the exercise is good but exhausting. No, that's it, enough – I decide I am going to see Hindley today, this afternoon, and no one is stopping me. I will just get a taxi there if I had to or ask Tilly to get me after she finishes her part-time job shift; she has offered to a few times but her parents didn't want her going near the prison. At least she's keeping me up to date when she can. She heard Leila is okay, and Stephanie has been undergoing recovery at her home with a specialist. She doesn't know Steph is an Immortalis, so it's interesting to hear what story the Saps are being fed.

Where are you, Heath? Answer my calls! Unless Edgar's not letting him into the house. Wow, I never thought of that. I walked to the enormous windows that took up one complete wall of the bedroom that I was in. If this was the guest suite, the main room must be something else. I leant against the window frame and looked out at the moors. I miss them. I could feel that soft wild grass around my ankles and smell the aroma of the earth. As soon as Isabella or Nelly showed up, I'd question them about Heath.

I only had to wait about ten minutes and Isabella, dressed in a label I recognise, swans in with a cup of tea for me. She obviously didn't do any part-time work at the family business during school holidays, maybe she just shopped.

I tried to join Edgar, Nelly and Isabella for breakfast, but Edgar liked to have it with me in my room alone before he went to work. Great, because I'm in there every hour of the day and that's just what I need! I sound so ungrateful.

She greeted me with a cheery smile. 'Oh good, I was worried I would wake you,' she said, and put the cup of tea down on the bay window seat near me.

'Thank you, Isabella,' I said, 'but you don't have to do that.'

'I don't mind,' she said, and stood opposite me to look out at the window. 'So pretty isn't it, but too cold to be out now.'

I looked at her and thought, there can't be two more different people in the universe than the two of us here now.

'Do you know if Heath has come by at all?' I tried to ask as casually as I could. 'I thought maybe Nelly was shooing him off until I was better,' I said sweetly.

She didn't meet my eyes. It was really weird.

'Um, he's been by a few times,' she said. 'Now, I'm going to the library this morning, would you like a book?'

She turned away and I put a stop to that.

'Isabella, please tell me, I need to know.'

She turned back to me and sighed. 'He's been here three times but not to see you,' she said, and blushed.

My mouth dropped open. So this is his game. He's either using Isabella to get to see me or he's using Isabella to punish me for going home with Edgar. I could tell she liked him and liked him a lot. Her eyes just lit up at the mere mention of his name, and she looked so coy.

'Isabella,' I said softly, 'be really careful. Heath, well, he's not boyfriend material, he can be wild.' I tried to say diplomatically he wasn't for her. I wanted to say that he was not interested in her in the least and was just playing her.

'I'm not looking to get married tomorrow, Cathy,' she said, and laughed. 'Besides, he's lovely and can be quite charming.' The smile lingered on her face, and she looked outside again.

'He's playing you,' I said, with less diplomacy than I should have.

She snapped to look at me and she was not happy.

'Of course he is. He couldn't possibly like me, only you. Funny then that he hasn't asked to see you!'

I bit my tongue from getting too carried away in the heat of the moment. I was the Linton family guest after all and dating her brother.

'I'm not saying he didn't want to see you, but he's angry that I'm seeing Edgar and—'

'You're just jealous, Cathy,' she said, cutting me off.

She strode out of the room then stopped in the doorway when I called after her: 'Does your brother know he's been here?'

The usually docile Isabella surprised me by saying: 'I'm sure my brother would be unimpressed that you asked after Heath before asking after your brother.'

'Well I know where Hindley is,' I snapped back. This wasn't going well. I was biting the hand that fed me. I softened. 'I'm sorry Isabella, you're right, Heath is all yours. You're beautiful and kind, of course you attracted him.' I turned back to the window.

I saw her in the window's reflection as she stood there looking at me for a moment, unsure whether to say something supportive or doubt my sincerity. She turned and left.

My tea was cold, and so was my heart.

*****

Heath

'Status quo and business as usual?' I asked, looking at the surrounding faces.

'I'd be lying if I didn't tell you we are pleased, and relieved too,' Edgar said.

We sat in the Mortuary Boardroom with his directors, and Mr Linton was on speakerphone from Rome. I had the four directors from the winery and blood wine company with me but not my blood bank staff, Conrad and Miles – they were Saps and this meeting was about blood.

I smiled and nodded my thanks to Edgar. I wanted to grab him and smash my head against his, tell him to keep his hands off Cathy, but I'm separating business from pleasure, and that would be a pleasure.

‘I’m pleased too, as you can image,’ I told the group. ‘I didn’t expect to be running the winery and blood wine arm of the business so soon, although I feel like I’ve been in training for it forever. Plus, I don’t want all of my father’s work dismantled.’

‘We’re grateful you want to stay with the existing contracts, Heath. They’ve been in place for over a century,’ Mr Linton said, ‘and I believe they are fair, I hope you feel the same.’

‘I do,’ I said, and I really did. ‘We both need each other and why try to change something that’s working perfectly.’

‘I’m not sure how we can contribute to the blood bank now,’ Edgar said, ‘if all of our supplies are going to the winery.’

I nodded. ‘Perhaps if we operate in organs down the track,’ I suggested. ‘Saps are running it, so I need to be careful, but I will bring in some Immortalist staff shortly,’ I told the group.

All the directors looked pleased with this.

‘Blood, a clever investment,’ Mr Linton said.

‘I don’t see the blood bank stocks affecting the relationship with the Mortuary at all,’ I told them. ‘And if we need extra stock, the winery will purchase the blood from the blood bank.’

‘Great,’ Edgar said. ‘That might solve some problems with top-shelf shortage.’

We bantered for another ten minutes, and then we were out of there and back to the winery. I can’t believe I’m in charge. Everyone has been so happy for me; part of that is the pure relief of not having to deal with Hindley. A lot of them have known us both since we were kids. Bizarre how it all just came together.

As for Cathy, I can't think of her without grinding my teeth. I can't believe she's over in that house and with Nelly too. Fuck. You'd think this would bring us closer – our chance to be in the house together, to run the business how Dad would have liked and to plan for our future, and she's over there in that soppy place. And if she seriously thinks I'm going to see Hindley and give him blood, she's taken a massive hit to the head. I want to see him, but just so I can sit on the other side of the bars and watch him shrivelling up and dying. I know how that sounds, but you can't abuse someone all their childhood and then expect to be best buddies. It will never happen. Never.

*****

Hindley

Even the rats know to avoid my cell now, since I've drained a few of them and thrown them out through the bars of my window. Talk about the lowest of the low and hardly top-shelf stuff, but survival demands it.

The guard locks me in with the solicitor again.

'How are you, Hindley?' Maurice asks, as if it is not obvious that I'm shit. 'Has anyone come in to see you?'

I know what he is asking, and he subconsciously covers the two telling penetration marks on his wrist where I fed. It was good of him to give me blood, especially since he'd feel it a lot more than an Immortalis. I willed him not to feel it so it would only be an after sting.

'Daniel's been up every second day,' I said, my tongue running over my teeth. 'He was going to organise a blood roster of visitors but nothing is happening.'

Maurice is studying me, but I can't look at him and talk to him at the same time. It's the blood pumping and the vein in his neck.

I continue. 'It's not easy drinking at breakneck speed or getting that camera covered and uncovered if I want to go the neck.' I nod towards a camera in the corner.

'I don't want to alarm you, but have you thought about how you would handle this if you got sentenced?' he asked me.

I feel my jaw tighten because he's skirting the actual issue. I rise and walk to the bars so I can watch him and talk to him from a safer distance.

'Truth is Hindley, the village is supporting you, but the second victim's family are causing quite a stir. As I mentioned last visit, his wife for reasons unbeknown to any sensible person, is defending her deceased husband despite his domestic violence record; his kids love him; his parents say he is the best son to walk the earth and his friends have lost a mate. You get the picture,' he finished.

'So worst-case scenario at a guess?'

'Under ten years,' Maurice says.

I bend over in shock and exhale.

'I won't survive. I'll die in here,' I tell him and straighten up. I begin to pace. 'Where's Cathy?'

'She's called me every day and is hoping to get up to see you soon. She's staying at the Lintons.' He shakes his head. 'She said the wellness police won't let her out.'

I try to smile but it's more of a scowl. I need her fucking up here now, and I need her to organise a blood roster.

Maurice pulls a large white handkerchief out and places it next to him on the desk. 'Hindley, drink now and make it quick,' he says.

I don't need to be asked twice. In a blur faster than the Saps' eyes can see I've covered the camera with the handkerchief, taken from his neck, drunk and pulled away long before I wanted to. The handkerchief was off the camera and back on the desk in moments.

'Thank you,' I said.

He nods and touches his neck. I can see he hates this.

Later, in my cell, I realise I have two options. I can stay, see through the sentence and either die in here of dehydration or become a shell of myself until I'm released. If it is longer than five years, I can't imagine anyone bringing me blood for that long… I'll just be living off vermin. Or I can get myself checked into the hospital ward and escape, which wouldn't be hard with my strengths. But then I can never come back to the village, and never come back to Wuthering Heights until everyone associated with the case has lived out their lives and died. Now, that might feel like forever – leaving my home and friends, but in the centuries to come that I will see in, it is but a minute in time.

Chapter 27 – Escape

Catherine

It's 10am, no one is home at the Linton household, thank God, and I'm getting out of here. God knows where Isabella has gone and who cares – a car just pulled up and she left with a friend, Nelly has gone to get some groceries, and Edgar is at work. I write a quick note:

Have gone to see Hindley. Will get a taxi back, please do not panic, I am fine! Love Cathy x

I leave it on the kitchen bench and grabbing my bag, I head out. It strikes me I really don't want to come back. It's not that I'm not attracted to Edgar, I am, but I want to go home where I can think clearly about what I want. I head out through the front door, down the driveaway, press the button on the large iron gate with the family crest on it, and close it again. In a few moments I'm on the moors; no one can see me and I can breathe.

I've missed you! I tell the moors and they respond with a

breeze and the smell of fresh earth. I know I can't walk the whole way but I want to walk through to the main road, to have some time on my moors, and then I'll call a taxi. I don't get any great pace up, every time I tread on something jarring my whole body feels it, but I don't care, I'm free, I'm home. The open land in front of me is medicine for my soul. I stop for just a minute to take it all in, then continue plodding along. I look like a zombie someone let out of the cemetery. I know the moors can take on many moods and some people fear the space, but not me. It is as comforting as Wuthering Heights. Now the ocean, that's something to be feared if you ask me!

I can see the road below now, so I grab my phone and call for a taxi to meet me at the corner near the road sign. I wasn't waiting long before I saw the car coming; the driver was Mr Elgee, his son Jared was in Heath's grade last year at school. I wave him down and get in the front passenger seat.

'Hello love, alright?' he asks. He's a big man, warm and friendly. I think he knows everyone in the village.

'Hello Mr Elgee,' I greet him. 'Thanks for picking me up.'

'Going to see Hindley, are you, love?' he asks and saves me from saying it.

I nod and tear up. God, I'm pathetic. Mr Elgee turns the car and we head towards the village and the small jail at the back of the police station. They won't always keep Hindley there, but for now, it's good he's local.

'You've had a rotten run, young lady, but hang in there… it's a lucky dip, you know,' he says.

I laugh at the thought. 'I've drawn a few crappy things out,' I agree, and he smiles.

'Aye, but think of what good stuff is still in the bucket for you, hey?' he grins and gives me a nod. 'I tell you, love, there have been some dark times during my life but I've always thought something good will come next, and it did, it always does.'

I dab my eyes with a tissue from my purse and thank him.

'How's Jared going?' I ask, putting some cheer in my voice.

'The lad is going great,' he said, expanding with pride. 'I tell you, love, if I wasn't at the birth, I'd swear the fairies left him... such a bright and kind boy. Doesn't get that from me, must be all from his mother.'

'I think he might be his father's son, too.' I smiled at him.

'He's doing well at his studies, and he's loving college. I hear young Heath is doing well too, always was a serious lad with a good head on his shoulders.'

I nodded, thinking it odd as I've heard no one's perception of Heath, but I guess Mr Elgee was right. Heath studied hard, studied the business, and was a pretty serious kid.

'You know Hindley's become a bit of a folk hero around here; lots of folks, parents like me, aren't too upset that the drug seller is off the street and as for the wife basher, well let it be a lesson to all.'

'I hope the judge or jury feels that way,' I said, and then the police station and prison came into view. I felt my chest tighten.

Mr Elgee pulled up at the side, not right out the front, bless him.

'Are you going to be okay, love, I can come in with you?' he said.

'Thank you, Mr Elgee, that's really kind, but I'll be fine.' I reach for my purse.

'The winery has an account. I'll just put it on that, hey?'

'That would be perfect, thank you.' His fatherly concern for me made me miss Dad terribly at that moment, not that I don't miss him all the time.

We say our farewells, I sent my best to Jared and alighting, I watch Mr Elgee drive off. *Righto, on with it then*, I coach myself and walked across the road. The prison was small and housed about ten prisoners, but at least locals don't have to go too far to see imprisoned relatives. God, whoever thought I'd be visiting here.

I brush down my jeans and black hoodie which had scored a bit of grass and weed from the moors, and with a deep breath, and a wince, I pushed open the door and headed in. I see a policewoman at the desk behind a glass barrier and a waiting room with a drink machine, a dozen chairs, a toy box and a TV which was on with the morning show and a commercial selling an inflatable mattress that can fit perfectly under the bed when stowed away. Good to know.

I go to the front counter and it never occurred to me there would be visiting hours, but now I see the sign on the wall.

'Can I help you?' the policewoman asks. She's about her mid-thirties and smiles at me.

'Hi, sorry, I didn't think about visiting hours. I'm here to see my brother, Hindley—'

'Earnshaw,' she says, cutting me off.

I nod. 'I'm his sister, Catherine.'

'Righto,' she says, and disappears for a moment below the counter level, rising with a clipboard, a pen and about 570 forms, okay, maybe three, in her hands. She passes them through the gap in the panels.

'First offender, huh?' she gives me a smile and a nod at the sign on the wall. 'You've got a forty-minute wait until visiting time but if you fill these in, that'll kill some time.' She flushes slightly, as though saying the word 'kill' probably wasn't the best idea in prison when I'm here to visit a murderer. 'There's a machine over there if you want a cold drink, and a kitchenette and toilet just down the hall if you want to make yourself a tea or coffee.'

'Thanks for all that,' I say, taking the forms. I need to sit down now. I'm aching all over, but I grab a cola first for a caffeine hit and then work my way through the paperwork. Soon a couple of other people arrive who were obviously in the 'know' about visiting hours – an older woman, a young guy, and later, a woman with a baby. We all greet each other with a nod and smile. No one wants to be here.

*****

Hindley

It's visiting hours and every day I sit here waiting and hoping. The guards come and get us if we have a visitor and we go into a large shared room. Most of my fellow inmates are here for pissy stuff like theft, drunk and disorderly behaviour, assault. I'm the only murderer. They give me a lot of freedom though, even taking the handcuffs off when I'm in the general area with visitors. I'm guessing if I hadn't killed two people that the cops were trying to lay charges on for a long time, they wouldn't be so generous.

They have taken me out of my cell five times in eight days to meet with visitors; you don't realise how much it means to the dicks like me locked up here until you're one of them. The guy next door goes every day, his wife and kid always come in. The old guy further up gets a visitor most days – his wife and kid or both. Daniel has been my only visitor. Maurice, my solicitor, doesn't count, and he doesn't have to come during visiting hours.

The guard parades past me with an inmate going to the visitors' room, and then he comes back for me. Fan-bloody-tastic. What I'd give to drink that whole room dry. I could do it of course but that would be the end of me and it would endanger everyone in our culture… which at this point I've got to confess I don't give a shit about, except for Daniel and Cathy.

'You're in luck today, Earnshaw,' the middle-aged guard says to me, 'a pretty young lady.'

Cathy! About bloody time. We head up the hallway and into the room, and everyone stares at me. They always do – rich kid turned bad kid; or hero vigilante, depending on where you stand. And there she is. I drop opposite her in the chair and we say nothing.

She tries to not look shocked at seeing me, but she looks just as bad. Cathy takes my hand, then when I shake my head, she withdraws.

'Too close, the blood,' I mutter, and she nods. 'Where have you been? What's wrong with you, you look like shit.'

She laughs a dry, not funny laugh. 'I've been sick, I got knocked out,' she reminds me, like I didn't know. 'Hindley, you look drawn. Are you getting any fluids?'

She uses a word that won't arouse any suspicion.

'Only when Daniel and Maurice come in and only what I can grab in the briefest moment.' I look around. 'It's impossible for me to get any from you here and now.'

'Can't you collapse and we can get you to the hospital? Say you need a transfusion or something?'

I look around, lower my voice, and move in closer to her. Luckily the kid opposite is squealing on his father's knee and everyone's watching and smiling at him.

'I can't do that for the next five or ten years, depending on my sentence. I either have to get off the charge but Maurice says that won't happen and there'll be some time served, or I need a regular blood supply, or I have to escape.'

'Could we try for home detention, community service, all that stuff?' she asks.

I laugh at the thought. 'Yeah, that'd be brilliant, but despite the community support, the cops will not want to set a precedent that you can kill whoever you want as long as they are a bad person. They might use me as a scapegoat example of why you shouldn't take the law into your own hands.'

She runs her hands through her hair and rests her chin on her hands. I can see her wrists and the faint blue veins. Cathy notices and pulls her arms off the table. I'm screwed.

*****

Catherine

He looks awful, truly awful, and seeing my reflection in the glass I look related. Mum and Dad would die all over again if they saw us now. How did we get to this place in time? I run through a hundred scenarios in my head, trying to play rescuer.

'If you are in here for any length of time, we're going to have to get someone in the jail kitchen to give you blood wine,' I whisper. 'They can dress it up however they like, beetroot soup, whatever, but we need an Immortalis in the kitchen.'

He nods. 'I'm working on a bigger plan than that.'

I groan. 'Please Hindley, don't do anything crazy, think it through.'

'Cathy, all I can think about is blood,' he says, and he glances at my neck again.

'Do it,' I say. I take off my hoodie and placed it next to me on the table.

He takes a deep breath.

'Too many in here,' he mutters and licks his lips.

'I'll stay right until the end, the last minute, and hopefully, we'll get a minute or two alone when everyone is saying goodbye,' I tell him. 'Or, drop your head onto my hand as though you're upset and crying… drink.' I put my arm out flat on the table and it happened. Hindley took my arm in both hands and lowered his forehead to my wrist as though in tears. I waited for the guard to say "no contact" but they didn't. The Saps wouldn't realise what was happening until it was over – it was a blur of speed. I could feel him drinking, that terrible feeling of blood being taken out made me feel weak, well weaker. Thank God it was super quick.

He covered his mouth with his hand as he lifted his head. I closed my eyes, letting the wooziness pass.

'Thanks,' he said.

I open my eyes and give him a weak smile. 'You look a little better already.'

My wrist was stinging and I can see two fresh marks there, but there's also bruising from the fall and other marks where the IV drip went in before.

'When is Daniel or Maurice next in?' I asked.

'Dan's here tomorrow, not sure about Maurice,' he says. He looks better. 'Oh God, I could have drunk you dry; it took all my self-restraint to pull away.'

'Yeah, glad you did,' I said, and he grins. 'I'll come the day after so you've got something to drink for the next two days.'

He nods and thanks me. And then visiting hours are over. I watch him taken away, can't believe it, and then out in reception I message Tilly to see if she can meet me in her lunch hour. Moments later, she messages back, 'we're on.'

*****

We sat at a corner table outside in the winery café, away from customers so that Tilly could have a break, and we ordered lunch. It was so good to see her and ride on some of her energy. She even gave me a bit of an appetite and we ordered fresh juices and chicken burgers with the lot.

'So, Leila is getting around on crutches but reckons she'll be back at school on Monday, but no-one has seen Steph,' Tilly says.

'I heard Steph had gone away to Switzerland to a health resort to recover,' I add to the discussion, knowing full well she had undergone the Conversion and was lying low. She could be anywhere but she'd have to give it a couple of months before she surfaced again given her injuries… the Conversion would heal them instantly and that would be hard to explain.

'It's great to see you,' I told Tilly.

'You too. I really appreciate the holiday work at the winery, but I miss not having you here. Great, I'm starved,' she said as Suzie placed our lunch in front of us.

We thanked her, and I ate like I hadn't eaten for a week. I just left everything outside the door for one hour and was there in the now with Tilly.

'And Jace?' I asked.

'Haven't seen him much. He went off to the coast for a few days with his folks, and I think Isabella has given him the flick. I heard she was seeing Heath again,' she said and looked to me for confirmation.

I shrugged. 'I haven't seen him. You're probably seeing more of him here at work than I have. But I'm heading home today.'

'I've seen him twice from afar, but we just waved and didn't get a chance to talk. I've got a date with Sean on Saturday.' She grinned, which made me grin.

'Sean and Tilly sitting in a tree…' I sang and she laughed.

'You're an idiot.' She rolled her eyes.

'Am too,' I agreed. In so many ways!

Chapter 28 – Full moon on the moors

Catherine

I felt so good after meeting with Tilly and just talking about school stuff, not all the other drama in my life. Tilly and I agreed we'd get a group together and hang out at my place on Friday night – movies and pizza. She's going to ask Sean and I'll invite Jace, Natalie and her guy, and a few others. It will be great. The fresh orange juice and food also helped, so I decided to walk home along the moors, back to Wuthering Heights, to my room. It's only just after one o'clock, and it doesn't matter how long I take. Besides, the exercise is supposed to be good.

I clear my mind and put one foot in front of the other. It was a perfect Autumn day, there was a crispness in the air, and the soft long grass swayed around me. It was sunny when I first started, but the wind was rising and it was clouding over. That was no surprise for the moors where you could have four seasons in four hours.

I passed through the grouped houses that were together at the edge of the moors before it became starker and more open – the part I loved. With the vigilante caught, everyone in town relaxed again. Well, everyone who might not have led a respectable life!

I walked for close to an hour and then felt exhausted. I sat on some low-rise rocks, looking over the valley and watched the clouds tumbling in. The wind was rising now, moaning gently in my ears – a sound I knew so well. I lay back on the sun-warmed rocks and closed my eyes; it was so peaceful.

I must have fallen asleep, my body was desperate for it, and I don't know how long I was out for, but raindrops woke me. I sat up alarmed and winced in pain; it was dark and gloomy; the wind was howling and sheets of rain were coming across the moors towards me. I would be cold, drenched, and not able to walk any further in a matter of moments, but I wasn't scared. I grabbed my phone from my bag and saw that it was nearly five p.m. – I had been sleeping for over three hours. Wow, I must have needed that.

I walked as fast as I could. There was a small cave ahead to huddle in; Heath and I had hidden in there many a rainy day on the moors. Despite the ache in my legs, the pain roaring up my back and neck, I kept going as fast as I could. The cave was nearer now. My imagination could see a younger Heath there. I suddenly missed him terribly – his strength and complete love for me. I'm such an idiot, who would throw that away? Why am I not content, why do I want more than I have? Is that normal?

Then the rain came down. It didn't just rain, it teemed, hard and fast, like needles into my skin. The wind was whipping around me, making it impossible to see one step ahead of me. I love and know the moors, but I know them well enough to know they don't have favourites – they were unpredictable and not that welcoming of human spirits amongst them.

I kept going, my head bowed to the weather, gasping in the air despite my hair being whipped around and the wind pushing against me. I stumbled over a small rock and hit the ground hard, pain shot through my already injured arm and ribs. Oh my God… excruciating. I thought I was going to faint. I didn't move for a few minutes until my eyes cleared and I could see again. I pushed myself up and kept going, almost there. Now soaked, my body aching and freezing, there was no way I was going to go back to Thrushcross Grange with all of them telling me how wrong I was to go out and how I was to stay in bed. No!

I tripped again just near the entrance; I was so close I could touch it. My bag, my clothes, my shoes, everything was soaked. I dragged myself on my knees to the cave entrance and climbed in. The relief was palpable. It was quiet in here and dry. I pushed myself up against the wall and sat looking out at the storm. I wished Heath was with me.

*****

Heath

Nelly called me and said Cathy had gone to see Hindley and had not returned home. Nelly had gone back to Wuthering Heights to look for her, but she wasn't there either, and now the storm was wild. I told her to wait at Wuthering Heights and not to worry, if she was on the moors, I knew where to look.

Cathy, Cathy, my Cathy, what are you doing? I grabbed some wet weather gear for what it was worth and headed out into the storm. The wind and rain belted me; I couldn't imagine Cathy with her already battered body battling this. I tried to see as far as I could despite the weather and the fog that had moved in, but my only real chance was to smell her scent, and I would know that scent anywhere. Prior, the wind carried the smell of her lavender and powder perfume to me but today the rain was a hinderance.

I went as fast as I could without completely taking my wolf's form… I wasn't too confident doing that in the daylight just yet. I came to one of our hideouts; I crawled into it and enjoyed the short reprieve from the rain and howling wind. I could tell and smell straight away that she hadn't been here. If she was coming from the village, she would have come along the waterfall route, but not knowing what time she left the jail, I wasn't sure how far along she would have got.

I forced myself back out into the storm and rushed along; the wind was now on my back – I appreciated the push along. I eliminated another one of our rock hideouts and I only had to look across the rock bridge to know she wouldn't be in our cave there – the rising creek had swallowed it. *Please don't be in there*, I silently willed her.

That left one place – our little rock cave, a den that was high and dry in the middle of some huge boulders. I saw it before I could discover her scent, and then it hit me – her perfume, she was there. I hurried to the cave, skidding and slipping on the slippery rocks, mud and long grass, and I saw her, not far in from the entrance.

I raced into the cave; she was feverish, half asleep, but then she opened her eyes and looked at me.

'Heath,' she said and smiled weakly. She looked at me like she used to do when she loved me.

I picked her up, held her against my chest to warm her, and backing out of the cave, I ran across the moors using all my powers and not caring who might see me. I took her home to Wuthering Heights.

*****

Nelly fussed and pampered Cathy, banning me from the room until she had her in dry clothes, tucked up in bed and sipping tea. She dismissed me to my room to get changed. Finally, when Nelly went to heat some soup, she allowed me to enter the room at last. Cathy looked so beautiful lying back in the bed, her dark hair spread across the pillow. The wind rattled the windows and the rain was falling softly now. We were home.

'Hey,' she said, seeing me, and smiled. She put out her hand and I came over and sat beside her on the bed. I held her hand and stroked her hair. We sat in silence.

'Don't go back, Cathy,' I said after a while.

She looked up at me and then looked away. I pulled back and twisted to sit and look at her.

'Tell me you are not going back to Edgar and Thrushcross Grange?' I tried to control my voice when I really wanted to give her a good shake and tell her to wake up to herself.

'But you've been seeing Isabella,' she told me, what do you care what becomes of me, Heath?'

I ran my hands through my hair and rose to pace. She was the most infuriating person in the world. She broke into a spasm of coughing and Nelly rushed in, scolding me and pulling Cathy's blankets up around her.

'Now don't vex her, Heath, and you Cathy, just calm down. I'm going down to get the soup.' She clucked her tongue and left us.

I returned to Cathy's bedside and sat on the chair beside her bed. Leaning forward, I tried to read her face, her sincerity.

'You know Isabella means nothing to me,' I told her. 'It was just a way to come to see you.'

'It was a way to make me jealous and hurt me,' she snapped back, and she was right.

'Oh, like you are doing with Edgar. You don't think that is torture for me? You are so completely wrong for each other. What do you see in him except a shiny big house and a man who will be an adoring lap dog?' I asked, and I realised I'd probably gone too far and my words would make her angry.

Her eyes narrowed, and she glared at me. Even sick, she still had the strength to level me with one look.

'You and Edgar have both broken my heart, Heath! He thinks I'm a toy that must be petted and controlled, and you, you would leave me for a year and then bemoan that my love for you has changed! But look at you...'

She broke into a coughing spasm, burying her face in the blanket so that Nelly didn't come running. I passed her a glass of water; she sipped it and then lowered her voice to continue.

'Look how strong you are,' she hissed at me. 'You will live forever and I will be gone… then you will have a lifetime to live without me, not just one year!'

'Ha,' I scoffed, 'I go away to improve myself to be the man you need, I miss you every single day and I come home to find that what you told Nelly was true, you wanted to play the field and see what else is out there. Look what you've caught – a well-bred, rich guy. Good on you, Cathy!'

I attempted to rise but she grabbed my arm.

'Do you really love me, Heath? If you could leave me for a year, how long would it take after my death for you to find happiness elsewhere and forget me? Maybe you'll just remember me when you pass the cemetery or go to visit our father's grave and see mine there.'

My blood was boiling with anger and torment. 'Stop speaking of death, Cathy, we are going to be Immortalis together. Stop torturing me.' I pulled away and strode to the window. The howling wind was more comfort to me than Cathy.

'Do you know…' she continued, her eyes watching me intently. They seemed so much larger in her pale face. '… I went over and over all our conversations when you left last year, wondering what I had said, what I had done. I tortured myself with fear of what you heard, each word that I'd uttered to Nelly burnt into my memory.'

'And you don't think what you say to me now won't eat into me eternally? Don't speak of dying, of not being with me, or of choosing Edgar over me.'

She smiled and it was almost a cruel smile. 'I'm not wishing you to feel any greater torment than me, Heath. We can be miserable and bitter together, and not be together. What a fine couple we will be.'

Chapter 29 – The end

Hindley

I am dying. The irony is not lost on me – by undergoing the Conversion to become an Immortlis and live forever, it will be the very thing that kills me in this place. But I know what I have to do now; I've made my decision. I'll miss my life, my fortune, taking what is rightfully mine. But I will take it, eventually. We'll soon all be Immortalis and Heath should enjoy the now, because after this lifetime, I will be back. When no one is around to convict me, I'll be back to claim all that is mine.

*****

Edgar

Cathy is back at Wuthering Heights, but not for long. She doesn't want Heath with his fake airs and new fortune. Clean him up all you like, he's rough and wild, and she's a lady. That family would have been much better off if Mr

Earnshaw had left Heath in the gutter where he found him. But she'll be back here soon, queen of my home where she belongs. We will be happy here forever. What an empire we will run.

*****

Heath

I sneak into her room just to watch Cathy sleep. She is all I have ever wanted, a love for an eternity. We are so close to having it all – our home at Wuthering Heights, the business to run, no more pressure or hate from her brother, and now we just need to seal our love. At the end of the year, she will finish school and we can commit. We can plan our future and become Immortalis together. She stirs, and I slip out again and leave her to lie peacefully. I return to my room, but soon I will move into Dad and Mum's room, we both will. I look out at the window and feel a rush of power. The full moon is rising and the hybrid side of my soul feels full of power and joy. I am so close to having it all, but the only thing I want is Cathy.

*****

Catherine

I see Heath depart through the ajar door of my bedroom. I love him. I hate him too, but I love him more. I am so weary from the three men in my life who all want something

from me. I just want to be living in the moment, with no decisions, no commitments. I want to just be seventeen. No pushing, pulling, anguish and arguments. And then I realise how I will do it. I throw back the bed covers and move to the rattling window. It's a beautiful night on the moors. The rain has ceased, the wind is lighter now and everything is lit by the glow of a full and rising moon. So beautiful.
I decide I will have my Conversion earlier, now. It will heal me. I'll be strong, young and look as I do now forever.
I choose myself.

THE END

Thank you for reading Cathy and Heath's story on the moors. If you are ready for a hot new couple who are bound to fall in love if they can stop sparring, then keep reading to enjoy the first two chapters of *Team Lucas* now. Read on for a sneak peek…

Chapter 1

Lucas Ainswright, the sexiest man alive, captain of a national soccer league team, World Cup player and my pain-in-the-ass boss, was bellowing at me again through the thin walls of the guest wing attached to his beachside mansion.

'We're leaving in five.' He thumped on the wall.

'I know, I know, I've got it,' I muttered. It's not hard to be ready to go to his training session three days a week at four o'clock. In my twenty-one years, I've managed to get to a lot of places on time, regularly.

Lucas wasn't really my boss; his father paid me to be his 'minder' and Lucas had to put me up in the guest wing. Trust me, I earned every cent, but the bonuses were great. For every week I lasted, I got my weekly fee doubled – it made Lucas almost bearable.

I locked up my wing of the house, the beach 'pad' as I like to think of it, and waited by his white Lamborghini. I bet the well-endowed, leggy, blond supermodel that I spotted leaving earlier this morning would look good next to this car; I bet she looked good inside it; I bet he looked good inside… whatever, where was I?

Lucas appeared – tall and toned, his light brown hair falling in his pale blue eyes. In his team's navy and white training gear, he looked as if he was heading to a photoshoot for *Sportsbabe* magazine. Okay, there's no *Sportsbabe* magazine but if there were, Lucas would be on the cover. The tragedy of lusting for Lucas was that I knew a lot of less attractive guys than Lucas who were so lovely that they were more attractive than Lucas, if you get what I mean? Lucas could stick his good looks and his attitude in his posh mansion. I was happy with him as eye candy only.

'Ready early, *Minder*?' he said, giving me one of his patronizing smiles.

'Didn't want to keep you waiting, mucus, uh sorry. Lucas.' I smiled back. 'Can I drive?'

'No,' he said flatly.

I pouted. 'Odds are that I will never, ever, in my whole life, ever get to drive a Lamborghini. Ever.'

'That's probably true,' he said, 'and definitely not in the four weeks you're working for me.' He unlocked the speed machine and offered me one of his special smirks. He stopped before getting in. 'Okay.'

I looked up at him to see if he was having me on.

'Really? You're going to let me drive?'

He looked like he was going to have second thoughts.

'What's the worst that could happen?' I asked him.

'We could die,' he said.

He hesitated and then stood away from the driver's door. 'All right, you can drive, but take it easy.'

'Yes!' I internally screamed with delight so he wouldn't change his mind, and ran around the front of the car to his side.

'Don't drive it like me,' he warned. He opened the car door wider for me and I got in, accidentally displaying a lot of leg in my workout gear. He knelt down beside me and moved the driver's seat forward, leaning over me to adjust the steering wheel. His goddamn gorgeous face with the one-day stubble was a lip pout away from me. I inhaled.

'Are you smelling me?' he asked and pulled out.

'No, I'm smelling the leather of the car. Your bad head just happens to be in the way,' I retorted.

I was inhaling his divine Armani scent, but in my imagination I had done more than smell Lucas on the nights I lay in the guest wing in my big, white, lonely bed. In most of those daydreams, though, he wasn't allowed to talk or scowl, he just had to perform as well as he did on the field but in the bedroom and on me. I would score him for tongue work, handwork and yellow card him when he wasn't paying enough attention.

Don't think about it, I told myself. I took a deep breath and faked smelling the leather again while I got my heartbeat under control.

Lucas closed my door and walked around to the passenger side. I started the car up while he put the passenger seat back and slid in next to me, his long legs filling the space.

'Wait, wait,' I said, grabbing my phone out of my bag in the backseat. 'I have to get a selfie of me in a Lamborghini.'

'I'll take the pic.' He wrestled my phone from me. I posed

and he snapped the shot. 'You're a strange girl,' he said, returning the phone to me. I dropped it in my bag.

'Why?' I asked as I adjusted the rear-view mirror and snapped my new ride into reverse.

'You've been with me nearly two weeks now and not once have you snapped a pic of me, or you with me, like every other normal red-blooded girl would do. Instead, you snap a pic of a car. You've got too much of the X-chromosome,' he said.

I shrugged. Better than having too much ego, I thought. I pulled out of the driveway and took off. I made a purring sound, and Lucas looked over and grinned at me. He shook his head. I rarely saw him smile, not at me anyway.

'Ooh, your car mistress is wonderful,' I said.

'She is that,' he agreed, sitting back casually and looking gorgeous, damn him.

I wished I could line up every single person I've ever known along each side of the road and drive by right now with Lucas Ainswright next to me and me driving his Lamborghini.

'So, let's see how she handles.' I put my foot down and Lucas freaked out.

'For fuck's safe, slow down,' he yelled.

'Why? You don't,' I called over the sound of the stereo.

He turned the stereo off.

'Watch the corner,' he pointed out.

'It's way over there,' I said, speeding by it.

'The turn is next right,' he directed, his foot flat to the floor trying to brake from the wrong side of the car.

‘I know, I’ve got it,’ I said, and spun the Lamborghini around the corner. Ten minutes later I pulled up in the parking lot of his club’s training facility. Several members of the team were outside.

Lucas leaped from the car, fell to the footpath and kissed the grass. I heard an uproar of laughter from the club.

I got out and grabbed my bag. He staggered to his feet, took his sports bag from the back luggage space, and made a big show of taking the keys from me. *Men.*

But I’m getting ahead of myself.

Being Lucas’s minder was a fluke because two weeks ago I was just in the right place at the right time – or the wrong place depending on how you looked at it…

Chapter 2

'Move away from the chocolate,' I ordered myself. 'Let go of the remote, get off the couch and go for a run now.' There, that should do the trick... nope, still no action.

It's not like I'm a major sloth. I run every day but since I got suspended for two weeks from my part-time job for telling a client to stick something up their ass, and I'm on semester break from college, I've been super unmotivated. I've worked my way through *The Walking Dead* and I'm about to start the box set of *The Vampire Diaries*, again. I'm as torn as Elena – I thought I was one hundred percent for Damon, but now Stefan is stealing my heart. It's complicated.

Yeah, sure I could have got another part-time job for the college holiday break – my best friend Alice, who is studying event management, could have got me waitressing work in the coffee shop where she worked, but I'm over people big time. Big time! I was in my last year of studying sports physical therapy and I worked part-time as a drug tester... no, I can't get free samples, let's just put that out there and move on.

'Integrity sampling' it is called. Sounds noble but I rock up to the client's house, get them to pee for me, shove my sampling stick in the mix and hope it reads 'clear'. Sometimes I just do a mouth swab if that's what the paperwork calls for, which is much easier. Occasionally I have to take blood.

Last week when I visited my goth-like client after one of his all-night rock sessions – may the god of eardrums spare us all – supposedly I didn't have my 'can do' attitude with me. He was so high I had to pull him off the ceiling to get his pee sample. Then he tried to tell me he had just emptied the tank so sorry, but he couldn't do it again. We might have exchanged words. He locked me in the bathroom for a while… yep, I get all sorts and there was nothing to read but *Back in Black* goth magazine. Then when he finally answered his phone and found me on the other end of the line, reminding him I was in the bathroom, he let me out. I might have suggested that the container he was supposed to do his sample in went elsewhere; plus, I made a few other self-improvement suggestions too.

I've had some real princes, but the best was yet to come – Lucas Ainswright.

The phone rang.

*****

I turned on the television and flipped channels. There he was on the news; Lucas Ainswright – the new David Beckham they were calling him, except Lucas had light brown hair that was constantly in his eyes, and those eyes were seductively crystal blue. He was tall with solid shoulders and arms that you could swing on; a sleeve of tattoos featured on one arm and his slender hips led to muscly calves. The Santa Ana Saints – a national league soccer team – signed Lucas on a massive deal and he'd also just secured a multi-million-dollar menswear modelling contract with Bastion, one of the hottest labels out.

I was so absorbed watching Lucas on TV that I forgot I was on the phone until I heard my boss – who dishes out my integrity sampling part-time jobs – reminding me.

'Are you there?' he asked.

'What? Oh yeah, sorry, I was just studying the… um… potential patient.'

'Four weeks' work at this stage. I know you're suspended but I've convinced them you've earned this.' He laughed hollowly.

I watched the screen as Lucas stopped to sign some autographs as he walked from the field; yep, he looked great in those shorts. I bet he'd look great out of those shorts too.

'Spill it,' I said. 'What's the deal?'

'Strictly confidential,' my boss said.

'Sure,' I answered.

'No seriously, this is strictly confidential,' he reiterated.

'Okay.' He sounded so serious that he had my attention now.

'Lucas Ainswright is the hottest ticket in town. He's got a three-year contract with the Santa Ana Saints, he's twenty-six years old, current net worth is $85 million and he's got talent. He's got endorsements that will bring in half of that again almost. But if he's not snorting his career away, he's smoking it.'

'I can't even imagine what $85 million looks like,' I said, staring at the screen. 'Oh Lucas, you idiot.' I couldn't take my eyes off him or his team as they posed in their navy, white and gold uniforms in front of a huge media scrum.

'So, his father, who is British and rather old school, along with Lucas's management and his coach, has agreed that he needs regular testing – a minder for the season, you might say, starting with a four-week trial. It would be part-time.'

I sat upright. 'And you put me forward?'

'It's a bit more complex than that.' I heard him take a deep breath. 'He's just been named captain of the team, so the other players and reserves will look to him to lead by example and he'll have that pressure on his shoulders – more than he had last season – you know pressure is a major trigger for relapse. He's also a renowned party boy and womaniser.' My boss cleared his throat and kept the worst for last: 'and he's burned through five other minders already – male and female.'

'And you're thinking of me because of… why exactly?' I frowned and rose from the couch to pace as we spoke.

'Well, because I'm short-staffed at the moment and I've got someone who is more senior available but not able to start until next week.'

'Oh, great, thanks for the vote of encouragement.'

My boss laughed. 'I mentioned you to them, Mia, because you can handle yourself; the reason you're suspended worked in your favour. His father loved that you told the other client off and he gives you full permission to do so to his son.'

'Didn't the other minders tell Lucas to pull his head in?' I asked.

'No. I think you'll find Lucas can be rather intimidating.'

'I bet he's a bighead,' I muttered, turning off the TV and moving to look out my apartment window at the apartment block opposite. There was a glimpse of green I could see from the park down the street.

'Boss, while I appreciate the chance to ogle a gorgeous, famous sports star, I'm tired of the fight with idiots who can't get out of their own way to help themselves, and who will water my cactus?'

'It pays ten times your daily rate. You could make more in these four weeks than you will in six months with your regular clients.' He lured me in. 'His father also offers a bonus system if you keep his son on track.'

'I was just thinking it was time to get off the couch and get back to work,' I told him.

Read more of Lucas and Mia's story now! Team Lucas is available in ebook and paperback.

Also by Ally Adams

The Spies in Love Series

My Boyfriend the Spy:

Matilda Martin, newly single, is having a life change – a new job, a new city, and a new dating outlook. That's right, she is over smooth men. In fact, Matilda is taking it one step further; she is only interested in Mr Average from now on – a man who doesn't have women hanging off him, doesn't know all the pick-up lines and is 100 percent real. Besides, she's bound to be too busy for men with her new job in the communications team of the FBI.

Adam Cahill is tall, dark, handsome and a spy for a government agency. And he has just been dumped. Allegedly, according to his now ex-girlfriend, he is "all about work, constantly grumpy, and as much fun as a crisis meeting". Adam has given up on finding love – from now on, he's focusing on his career. His latest case is just a little creepy… an old fairground, a carousel that turns by itself at night and a street under attack.

Luckily Matilda's been assigned to his next project since neither of them is bound to be interested in each other.

I Spy My Guy:

Irish-girl Orla Murphy is a romantic – books, films, real life – she believes in love; she's just got to find it. Accepting a one-year contract to work in Washington DC as a translator, Orla leaves her Dublin hometown for a new start.

Nick Hughes is 100 per cent work-focused especially after his last relationship exploded along with his heart. He's made it clear he's not interested in romance, no matter who might catch his eye.

When Orla finds several old notes written by a child in her library copy of *Anna Karenina,* she decides to track down the owner and give them back. She soon discovers that the owner has been missing for decades and is filed as a cold case. Suddenly Orla finds herself with a mystery, the notes open up a whole new angle to the case, and Nick is assigned to work on it.

Now they'll have to see each other every, single day!

The Saints series:

Team Lucas

Just let me get my fill of you and I'll deal with the fallout if it happens... when it happens.

Mia Carter never thought getting suspended from her part-time job for having attitude could be the best thing to ever happen ... maybe. When Lucas Ainswright—one of the world's biggest sporting stars—needs a minder, it just so happens that attitude is needed to keep Lucas in line. Now Mia's job is to manage the sporting world's bad boy and keep him at the top of his game for the season. Game on!

Team Tomás

Tomás Carrera has had to be responsible all his life. Growing up with a single mom and as the eldest of five siblings, Tomás missed out on a childhood of his own. Now his superstar soccer status has provided for his family and allowed him to let his hair down... and that's just what he's doing. Signed to the Santa Ana Saints, Tomás is catching up for lost time with fast women, a fast Ducati motorcycle and a bevy of adoring fans. That is until he loses his heart to Alice and is torn between wanting her and his independence.

Team Niklas

In his hometown of Berlin, Germany, Niklas Wagner is a superstar and when the Saints' pay the big bucks to sign him up and bring him to Santa Ana, California, Nik takes a shine to his new life. When he meets the Saints' media officer, Sasha Saxon, sparks fly literally. But Sasha is not your average girl—by day she is a journalist who looks after the media for the national champion soccer team and at night she designs for her fashion label. She had big dreams and they don't include a boyfriend. Nik has never had to chase the girls, but now he has met his match—Sasha is about to lead him on the biggest chase of his life.

Team Alex – 'The Russian'

He's tall, dark, handsome and athletic and just that little bit mysterious. He's also over women, big time. A star of the Saint's team, Alex Renwick – nicknamed 'The Russian' – has had a high-profile relationship with a Hollywood director's daughter for years, and now that it is over, he just wants to focus on his sporting career. Carly Brooker's professional sporting career as a basketballer with the Suns is about to end due to injury. To mask the pain, she throws herself into developing her role as a sports reporter. There's just one problem, she needs a date for the Suns' Ball where she will announce her retirement. When these two sporting hotshots meet, they are more than a good fit; they are made for each other… if they can just file away the doubts they carry and find a way to be together.

Acknowledgments:

Thank you for reading and hopefully enjoying my vampires on the moor novel, *The Dark Moors.* I have long held a passion for the moors and for Emily Bronte's powerful classic novel, *Wuthering Heights* – the power and moodiness of the moors lends itself so perfectly to a generation of dark spirits.

I look forward to connecting with you and invite you to follow me on Facebook, Bookbub and Goodreads. And finally, thank you to all my favourite romance authors whose works keep me inspired and challenged!

About Ally:

I am an Australian journalist and writer, postgraduate qualified in Literature and Communications, with a diploma in Counselling! I've been so lucky to have worked in television, print newspapers, magazines, radio and online media. Now I just love writing at my home desk overlooking the park with my favourite romance programs streaming in the background and my beloved Boxer, Hastings, on the couch nearby.

Connect with Ally:

Website - http://www.allyadamsbooks.com/

Facebook: https://www.facebook.com/allyadamswriter/

Pinterest (where I pin my character inspirations and images):
https://www.pinterest.com.au/allyadamsauthor/boards/

Goodreads: https://bit.ly/2QhN50N

BookBub: https://www.bookbub.com/authors/ally-adams

Lightning Source UK Ltd.
Milton Keynes UK
UKHW012133110722
405718UK00004B/117